I0766913

The Water Nymph's Plaything
A Lesbian Spanking Fantasy Adventure

The Water Nymph's Plaything
A Lesbian Spanking Fantasy Adventure

By
Clarine Klein and Leila Hann

http://clarineklein.com

Fresh from her novice training as a sister of the Celestine Order, Sally Vinebrook travels the world in search of magical secrets to further her education in the arcane arts. Following up on a rumor, she comes across The Misty Bog, home to an ancient and powerful water nymph named Modan.

After begging for a chance to study with her for a time, and a very thorough spanking for being so disrespectful to her swamp upon arrival, she is shown a brand new world of magic unlike anything she's ever known!

Though by the end of her stay, she just might not be able to sit down ever again.

Chapter 1

The Lady of the Mist

Clip… Clop… Clip… Clop…

Slowly and deliberately, Sally Vinebrook eased her horse along the narrow path that snaked its way in a meandering zigzag through the heart of the massive forest that blanketed countless leagues of the Western Reaches. Though the pace was slower than either of them would have preferred, both rider and mount were content to take their time and ensure that each step was placed on solid (well, solid *enough*) ground; doing their best to keep a wary eye out for snares and pitfalls, or anything that might think diminutive mage girls made for tasty snacks.

After all, becoming dinner for some nameless horror that lurked in the bowels of the forest was no way to go about having an adventure. Which was exactly what she was *trying* to do!

Sally Vinebrook was on a quest for knowledge. More specifically, she was looking for a spring. But not just any spring. She was looking for a *mystical* spring. She'd heard second and third-hand accounts at a local inn some three days' ride back about a squire boy who had inadvertently stumbled into the domain of a water nymph here in this very forest, and now she was determined to do the same.

The lucky lad had even had the good fortune of actually coming face to face with the mistress of the bog herself! Apparently she'd made quite the impression on him, because everyone Sally had spoken to at the inn had been more than eager to recount his adventure for her once it had become known that she had the coin to pay for the information in drinks. Unfortunately, the details of what *exactly* had happened between the boy and the naiad had been murky, and often rather contradictory, and in the end what little she'd managed to pry from the locals had sketched only a very basic picture.

Somewhere deep in the forest, nobody could say for certain other than that it was near its heart and required at least two or three days of careful riding to reach, there was a bog, within which apparently lived some sort of water nymph.

Beyond that though, the rest was speculation.

While the story itself wasn't exactly up to her mistresses' usual standards of academic rigor, Sally still felt confident that she'd managed to spin the tenuous threads of rumor that she'd gathered during that night of unsupervised drinking and fact-finding into a reasonably compelling – and brief – report, which she'd sent with a letter carrier back to the monastery before she'd set off. Hopefully it would be enough to keep the locals from thinking she was off on some wild goose chase.

Bunch of porridge-minded rock farmers… Humph!

The thought of the nearby townsfolk's complete and utter lack of any proper documentation of the boy's adventures into the bog were enough to make Sally's blood boil as she twisted her reins in frustration. How could they not understand what a fantastic opportunity for learning that had been? Were encounters with creatures of legend so commonplace for them that they just didn't care? It was absurd!

Fuming to herself over all the valuable information that may have been lost forever because of their ignorance, she gave the sides of her mare a sharp little kick with her heels, and was rewarded with an equally sharp snort and buck of the animal's hips that bounced her roughly in her saddle.

"Sorry Bella," she sighed in apology, leaning forward and patting her steed behind the ears, making sure to rub the knot underneath the left one that always made her swish her tail happily.

"Get a hold of yourself Sally," she chided herself quietly. "You're supposed to be a proper and in control acolyte now, not some unruly novice!"

Shaking off her annoyance and fixing on a chagrinned smirk, grateful that nobody had been around to see her moment of petulance, she smoothed down the front of her tan tunic across the ample swell of her chest and refocused her thoughts on the task at hand.

The important thing was that there *had* been a boy who'd ventured into the naiad's domain somewhat recently, and that said boy had escaped (or rather, had been allowed to leave) from the bog alive. That indicated to her that the mystical entity that had dominion over the area did in fact exist, probably, and that she wasn't particularly malicious, probably. Or at the very least wasn't outright hostile toward humans.

Again, probably.

To be fair, she *had* heard a few accounts that included the boy fleeing from the swamp with a bright red bottom and no clothes on save for his boots, but that didn't sound all *that* scary.

As a newly elevated sister of the Celestine Order, having just completed her novice training only a few weeks earlier, it was her responsibility for the foreseeable future to explore the world in search of new lore and training on her own before returning home, which meant facing the possibility of a little bit of danger. Turned loose from the monastery that had been her home for the better part of the last decade, she was beyond excited for any opportunity that might give her a chance to put the arcane arts she'd been honing day in and day out to the test, and if that meant stepping into the domain of some grumpy goose naiad, then so be it.

She'd just be on her best behavior.

While rumors of a water spirit who vented her frustrations on people's backsides and taking their clothes might have scared off other, less intrepid, adventurers than herself, it only served to draw in the young mage in like a moth to the flame. As a proud Cindertouched sister of the Celestine order (and a respectably powerful one at that, if her mistresses were to be believed), of course she was intrigued! Although the extent of her experience within the realms of the Watertouched extended only to her heating up her bath water at night, she still couldn't help but be fascinated. After all, it was a *naiad*. How often did someone get the chance to meet one of those in person?

Apparently not very, if the scant accounts she could recall coming across in the monastery's archives were anything to go by. At least, not in recent centuries.

The way she saw it, it was her responsibility as a sister of the Celestine Order to investigate and properly document this mystical bog and its elusive mistress.

For posterity.

'My Adventures into the Deep Dark Woods' sounds like a sufficiently impressive sounding title for this journey to me, she thought to herself with a giggle. *No, no, how about 'A Descent into Danger and... Darkness' instead? Yes, that's even better!*

Humming happily to herself as she pictured the looks on her former instructors' faces when they eventually read her account, Sally urged her steed to move a little bit faster.

"Come on, Bella, it can't be too far now."

And then, as if she'd been destined to find it all her life, she was suddenly there.

"Hmmm…"

Reining in her horse to a stop, Sally squinted her bright green eyes behind her delicate spectacles at an even more narrow and brambly path through the trees just a few paces off to her right. To any ordinary observer, it might have just looked like another small offshoot that led deeper into the forest, but Sally Vinebrook was no ordinary observer. She could *feel* the roiling currents of the Power thrumming from deep within the shroud of trees, radiating out in palpable waves that vibrated in her bones as her heart fluttered in excitement.

She'd found it!

Scrambling down from off the back of her horse, she nearly toppled into the mud in her haste to investigate the seemingly innocuous offshoot. She let out a giddy squeal of delight then as the soles of her soft leather boots came into contact with the damp earth beneath her, and overjoyed, she threw her arms around her mare in a fierce hug.

"We did it Bella, it's really here! There's an *actual* water nymph somewhere down along that path. There just has to be, I can feel it! Oh if only Mistress Alviren were here to see this."

The thought of her strict – but never unkind – former instructor sobered some of the young acolyte's exuberance, and with a burst of speed borne from years of quick swats to the seat of her apprentice robes to get her moving, she set to work lashing her horse to a tree so that it wouldn't wander off anywhere while she was exploring the bog. Then, after giving the matter some more thought, she undid the knot and petted her mane reassuringly.

She wasn't sure how long she'd be gone for, and she would just hate for something bad to happen to her mount just because she was stuck to a tree and unable to escape.

"You just wait here for me, alright?"

The horse gave a snort and a shake of its dappled mane, and Sally patted her affectionately on the cheek again.

"Good girl."

After securing an overstuffed feedbag of oats around Bella's muzzle so that she could enjoy a well-deserved snack while she rested, Sally took in several long, deep breaths to steady her nerves and gave her tunic and riding pants a few quick tugs to make sure that she looked presentable. Then, gathering her courage and thrusting her shoulders back, she stepped onto the path that led away from her horse and deeper into the dark forest.

"I should be back before nightfall, Bella," she called in a sing-song voice over her shoulder as she disappeared into the press of trees. "Be good for me while I'm gone, alright?"

As she moved forward, the trees around Sally began to grow fewer in number, but thicker and older. Their canopies formed a roof of leaves overhead with some branches brought low under the weight of many hanging vines and other strange growths, all of which pressed in above her to blot out the sun's light so that only a faint trickle was able to find its way through. Underfoot her boots made muffled squelching noises as they tread tentatively across a thick carpet of damp leaves and springy undergrowth, and as she continued to follow the winding path for what felt like forever, a heavy white mist began to crawl across the forest floor toward her, further obscuring her vision.

On the bright side though, it was nice and warm, and the growing heat and moisture buoyed her spirits.

She was getting close.

Weaving her way around a pair of thick, root-gnarled trunks, Sally let out a small gasp of excitement as she caught her first glimpse of a dark green pool of water filling a vast clearing ahead of her with more tree trunks sprouting up ahead of her on all sides like the pillars of an ancient temple. The fog here was heavier than it had been back in the forest and seemed to be rolling in from across the water, blocking her view of whatever was on the other side… or even in the middle. Stranger still, from somewhere further ahead beyond the fog she could hear a faint bubbling noise.

"Wow…" she breathed in a low whisper, momentarily overwhelmed by what she was seeing.

With a mixture of excitement at having finally reached her destination after several sleepless nights lying awake with her mind racing at the prospect of what she might discover, and trepidation at being well and truly alone in the domain of a powerful magical entity, Sally took a moment to once again gather her courage and straighten out her outfit before she moved forward.

Her spectacles began to fog over as she ventured closer to the shoreline of the murky green pool, and she had to pause every few paces to wipe them clean with the inside of her forest hued cloak. It was like walking through the inside of a bathhouse! The nearer she drew to the water, the more the humidity began to make her sweat, and about halfway to her destination she was forced to draw back her hood to expose her intricate bun of bright blonde hair to the somewhat cooler air around her. She could hear the bubbling sound in the distance far more clearly now, and she found herself idly wondering if perhaps something was boiling there beyond her sight.

It sure feels hot enough for that! she thought to herself with a nervous titter. *Plus it would explain where all of this mist was coming from…*

Aside from the steady, rhythmic churning of water in the distance, the bog itself was eerily silent.

Drawing near the muddy edge of the small lake felt to Sally as if she were stepping into the hall of worship for some long-forgotten religious sect, and she suddenly wasn't sure if she was supposed to be there. She did her best to try and ignore the sensation that she was treading on sacred ground uninvited that was currently gnawing at the pit of her stomach as she craned her head back in an attempt to catch sight of the tops of the trees surrounding her. Their reach was far too high for her to discern anything that might constitute a "top" in this mist, however, seemingly stretching on for eternity.

Do they even have a top?

Shaking off the thought, Sally brought her gaze back down to the lake in front of her, and with another deep breath began to center her mind, her senses reaching out to feel the energy of the territory all around her.

It was incredible!

But now came the hard part.

Clearing her throat, she drew herself up to her full height (for what little of it there was), and with as much confidence as she could muster, called out into the silence.

"Um, h-hellooooo! Is anybody home?"

Her words echoed across the still surface of the lake, only somewhat muffled by the thick, rolling mist.

For several long moments nothing happened, then just as she was about to call out again (only this time a little bit louder) she heard a sloshing sound just ahead of her and off to one side, like something heavy emerging from the thick, muddy water.

Giddy with excitement but managing to keep herself under control lest she look like an undisciplined novice, the young mage leaned forward eagerly and squinted behind her fogged-up spectacles into the mist ahead of her in an attempt to pick out what was doing all that splashing. Said noises quickly became sloshing footsteps, followed a moment later by heavy growling, as the form of a massive creature with two legs, no arms, and a *huge* mouth full of pointy teeth emerged from out of the mist and began to lumber ponderously toward her.

"Eek!" cried Sally, her bleary-eyed squint shattering into a mask of terror as she got a good look at the horned monstrosity heading for her with a hungry look in its three, beady little eyes.

Terrified as she was, at least part of her still remembered her training, and with trembling hands and a pounding heart she reached deep within the swirling ethereal energies all around her, gathering them to her chest in a concentrated ball of light as she cried out.

"I am not a snack!"

With that, she hurled the energy toward the monster, managing by some miracle to actually hit it. The haphazardly formed ball of Power made manifest flashed a brilliant shade of red as it sailed across the water and then exploded in a shower of sparks against the monster's rough hide. However all the attack seemed to do was scorch some of its scales and make it angry.

And that's when true panic began to set in.

Growling in pain and surprise, the beast stumbled around in a daze for a moment before regaining its footing. Then, lowering its oversized spine-covered head, its toothy maw yawned wide enough to swallow Sally whole, and with a thundering roar it began stampeding forward through the muck and fog, clearly coming in for a bite.

"S-stay awaaaaay!"

Realizing that she was about to meet a gruesome end at the

jaws of an even more gruesome swamp monster, she turned on her heel and started fleeing from the charging monster just as fast as her mud-caked boots would carry her.

"No, please, I'm sorry! Go away!"

As she slipped and stumbled her way away from the edge of the lake, nearly toppling into the mud on several occasions, the young mage desperately tried to calm her mind and channel a proper attack spell, or defense ward, or *something*. Unfortunately for her however, the real world was far less neat and organized than the archives and practice ranges back home at the monastery.

At least there none of her books ever tried to eat her.

Well, not usually.

Either way though, Sally was unable to channel so much as a spark of the Power right then, and with that horrifying realization came tears of frustration, streaming from the corners of her eyes and obscuring her vision as she continued to make a mad dash toward the tree line and its flimsy promise of safety.

Then, as if they'd never been there in the first place, the growls and sloshing footfalls suddenly stopped, leaving only the faint bubbling of water and the distant songs of frogs, birds, and buzzing insects in the distance.

"Oh dear, oh my… Oh gods below, forgive me for being such a fool! I *swear* I'll be more careful from now on…"

It took several more heart-poundingly terrifying moments for Sally to fully come to grips with the reality that she wasn't being chewed on by any rows of razor-sharp teeth, and it took several *more* moments for her to gather enough courage to peek out from behind the tree trunk she'd hidden behind.

The monster was gone.

"Creature." she chided herself, her mistress' sharp voices ringing in her ears despite the fear still roiling through her veins. "It was a *creature*, not a monster. Don't be silly."

Stepping out from behind her tree and retracing her muddy footprints back over to the edge of the shallow lake, she cast a long, searching glance in all directions before finally letting out a huge sigh of relief and collapsing unceremoniously onto her backside against the soft earth with a squishy *thump*.

It was gone. She was safe.

"Thank goodness…" she sighed, flopping back against the muddy shore behind her, ignoring how dirty it was going to get her clothes as she nearly started sobbing in relief. "That was *way* too close."

Then, as if in response to her, there suddenly came a deep, female voice from somewhere within the fog.

"Humans," it drawled in bemused contempt. "All the same these days. Trying to kill things for no good reason, even when you're unlikely to succeed."

The fog seemed to thicken as she spoke.

"She's hungry you know… Do you think perhaps I should let her eat you?"

"Wha-?"

The voice had Sally jerking back up in an instant, and although she could tell it was coming from somewhere within the thickly swirling mist that hung like a shroud above the water in front of her, she couldn't yet make out the figure of whoever was speaking.

Not that she really had to guess who it must be.

That commanding presence, that mellifluous cadence, the way the energies of the forest and water seemed to crackle with each syllable. It could only be the water nymph who made this bog her domain.

Scrambling back to her feet and hurriedly trying to brush away the mud and stray bits of leaves clinging to her sodden clothes as best she could, Sally squeaked nervously and replied.

"Um… I wasn't t-trying to kill it, ma'am!"

Then, gulping and fumbling for some excuse that would keep the mysterious nymph woman from turning the creature loose on her again, she added hurriedly.

"I wouldn't make a very good snack, anyway! But if you want, I could… I could, um… Oh!"

Her face lighting up in a smile as an idea came to her, Sally whipped around and began gathering the Power of the forest to her once again, this time focusing it on one of the trees near the shoreline as she said through a veil of concentration.

"I can… make this… tree… grow some delicious… fruits… instead..!"

And true to her word, the branches of the tree that she was focusing on began to writhe and snake, reforming themselves on a fundamental level as small, sweet apricots began to blossom and swell in bunches along them.

"Oh? And why are you making this tree grow delicious fruits?"

The voice seemed to be closer now, just beyond the wall of fog.

Her unexpected question distracted Sally for a few precious heartbeats as she looked back to cast her eyes about in search of the naiad again. Suddenly she couldn't help but feel as if she were back at the monastery and about to be chewed out for not knowing the answer to a question she'd been asked.

"Um, well…" she stalled, trying to come up with something sufficiently clever sounding.

Nothing was coming to mind though, and she could feel her mouth growing uncomfortably dry with each passing moment.

"S-so she can eat..?"

A furtive glance back at the tree she'd been manipulating caused her to realize that her lapse in concentration had allowed her blossoming fruits to wither to almost nothing on their branches. And with a terrified squeak, she redoubled her efforts, pouring as much energy into the tree as she could and causing the apricots to swell like bright orange balloons before suddenly bursting.

"Oh no!" she moaned, a wave of mortified horror washing over her as her face and hair were pelted with a hail of apricot debris. "Hold on, I can fix this!"

In response, a deep, melodious laugh reverberated across the swamp.

"I think I've seen quite enough of your particular brand of problem solving, little human."

More chuckles continued to echo all around her, and Sally cast another quick look over her shoulder toward the shoreline behind her before fully turning with a nervous swallow.

"But you're at least much more polite than the last one of your kind who came here was."

Only a few feet away from her now, she saw the silhouette of a head rise up out of the water. Although most of its features were still obscured by fog, she could still make out the impression of a strong chin, round, full cheeks, and thick, tangled hair falling behind its owner like a damp curtain.

"How about you don't accidentally destroy any of these trees, though?"

Feeling her cheeks coloring at having failed so spectacularly to impress the mysterious nymph, Sally released her mental hold on her failed apricot tree. In the distance she could just barely see the outline of the woman's face now, and the sight of those strong commanding features made her stomach flip-flop in the same way it so often did whenever Mistress Alviren would summon her to her chambers for…

Cutting her wandering thoughts off with a shake of her head and an even brighter blush, she clasped her hands in front of her and bowed in supplication.

"Oh please, *pleeeease* don't let her eat me, Mistress Nymph!"

"Mistress Nymph?" laughed the voice again, although this time it was more of a quiet giggle. "I am Modan, child. And *you* are a strange, funny little creature."

With those words the figure began moving closer, somehow not leaving a wake as she glided smoothly through the water and out of the fog toward Sally. As she approached the shore, she rose up out of the lake, giving the young mage her first clear view of the vinelets and little blossoms woven in throughout the curtain of dark hair framing either side of her wide, naked shoulders and round breasts.

Eying her back far more openly, the naiad's aquamarine hued lips twitched up into a teasing smile as water trickled down her belly and between her bare thighs.

"Were you looking for a wolf to skin to impress your little friends? Hmmm, no… I don't think so. Not this one…"

Modan reached up and pushed back a stray lock of hair with a little sigh, all the while keeping her liquid, dark eyes fixed on the stranger in her bog.

"But another human so soon? Surely that must mean something…"

Sally could feel her ears burning all throughout the naiad's inspection of her. She'd been *trying* to be polite and respectful, but the way the nymph woman had laughed off her earnest pleas to not be served as a snack just made her feel like a fumbling novice all over again. She didn't have much time to dwell on those feelings however, as she surreptitiously stole her first proper glimpse of the woman's form as a whole, her still stooped forward bow putting her precisely at eye-level with her more than ample chest.

She was *beautiful.*

Moreover there was something intangible in the fluidity and grace of her movements that belied the raw power she knew thrummed within her, making Sally swallow hard as her heart was set a flutter.

Gods below, I can't believe this is really happening!

It took a few moments before she finally realized that Modan had stopped speaking and was eying her expectantly. She'd been so caught up in staring at the enticing bare breasts on display before her (it was the first time that she'd had the opportunity to be so close to someone so… commanding in such an intimate way in a very long time) that she'd completely lost track of herself. Then, blushing scarlet, she piped up from behind her still-clasped hands (now hiding behind them like she had with the tree trunk earlier), squeaking.

"M-my name is S-Sally Vinebrook Mistress Nym-, I mean, Mistress Modan!"

Swallowing hard she forced her bright green eyes up to meet the creature's fathomlessly deep, black ones as she went on earnestly.

"I'm, uh… I'm a mage of the Celestine Order out on her first excursion from the monastery, and I… I heard that there was a water nymph that lived in this forest and I wanted to um… to meet her, and uh…"

She swallowed again then as she ran out of steam, eyeing the woman and hoping against hope that she'd believe her story and not think that she was plotting some sort of foul treachery. Then, remembering the packet of seeds she still had tucked away in a pocket of her cloak, she snatched the small pouch out and held it before her with slightly trembling hands as she added hastily.

"I um… I brought you s-some marsh marigold seeds as a gift, Mistress Modan!"

Not immediately speaking, Modan strode forward until she was looming directly before Sally, the waterline now at her ankles. Naked but for the curtain of black hair framing her face and chest, she seemed to tower over the diminutive mage girl both in height and mass as she plucked up the small pouch of seeds.

"Oh." she said with a thoughtful frown, rolling one of them between her damp, pale-skinned fingers. "These are like the herbs that grow near my banks… Like them, but still different."

She looked back at the still bowing mage with a softer, more appraising smile this time.

"These may be nice to grow."

Then, raising a dark eyebrow, she added with a smirk.

"Just so long as you leave the growing to me."

A chagrinned smile to match the water nymph's demeaning one tugged at the corners of Sally's lips, Modan's teasing admonition about "assisting" her plants along in their growth having hit far too close to home for her liking. She knew that she'd botched her earlier attempt to save her skin and impress her, which was doubly-embarrassing considering that coaxing plants to grow strong was ostensibly one of her specialties as a Cindertouched mage. The blow to her pride stung more than she thought it would, and she planned to redouble her drills from then on so that she could do better next time.

Assuming of course, there would ever even *be* a next time for her. That yet remained to be seen, unfortunately.

Straightening up from her bent over position and surreptitiously knuckling the aching small of her back while at the same time trying to take in every detail of the naked nymph standing in front of her without her noticing, Sally felt a fresh wave of nervousness seize her stomach.

Nodding shyly and doing her best to sound respectful and sincere she said, "I-I'm happy you like them, Mistress Modan, and um… I'm sorry I, uh… I'm sorry I couldn't help feed your, um…"

She gestured vaguely toward the wall of mist obscuring the water behind the naiad and gave her an embarrassed shrugged.

"Your pet."

"I don't keep pets… Although if you'd like to feed that hungry knucker, you still can," replied Modan with a cruel grin. "I don't think you actually want to do that, though."

"N-no that's fine!" Sally quickly reassured her with a frantic wave of her hands. "I *really* don't taste that good, I promise."

"Is that so?"

With her grin now firmly in place, Modan stepped out of the water and circled around to stand directly behind Sally, getting a good look at her from all angles.

"Well, you've met the lady of the spring, oh intrepid scholar of the arcane. What did you plan to do after that?"

She was still smiling as she spoke, and her deep voice had adopted a teasing quality now. Both of which were very good signs as far as Sally was concerned.

Feeling herself stiffen at Modan's words, the sight of her cruel grin sending frissons of nervous excitement coursing down her spine and making her stomach flip-flop, it took all of her willpower not to turn around just then. Instead, doing her best to keep track of the water nymph's presence through her powerful aura and out of the corners of her eyes, decades of Mistress Alviren's pre-discipline lectures keeping her feet rooted firmly to the ground and her back straight, Sally racked her brain for something to say.

Swallowing hard in an attempt to return some of the moisture to her suddenly dry mouth, she opened it to speak only to then realize that she really hadn't planned this far ahead.

Oh dear…

Clamping her lips shut again, she blushed and then a moment later offered weakly, "Um… I was rather hoping that maybe I could stay with you for a few days so that you could, um… teach me about yourself and your domain?"

Then, worried that she may have been too forward, she added quickly.

"I-if that's alright with you, I mean! If not I'll leave right now, and I promise I won't tell anyone about your bog, I-!"

Realizing that she was rambling, Sally snapped her mouth shut tight once again before any more foolish words could come tumbling out of it.

Modan didn't seem to mind though, her grin growing even wider as she stepped in close enough that the jittery mage could feel her body heat intermixing with the warmth of the rolling mist all around them.

"I don't know about a few days," she murmured very softly, making the younger girl's skin prickle as she strained to catch every word. "But a polite, respectful human who comes bearing such lovely… *gifts*…"

At that, she walked around behind Sally again, licking her aquamarine lips with a low chuckle.

"…would certainly be welcome to stay for a time."

"Really?" asked Sally, not daring to let herself hope as the butterflies in her stomach grew all the more agitated.

Her composure was also strained by the fact that she could feel the nymph's hot breath on the back of her neck and shoulders.

"Sure," replied Modan matter-of-factly as she breezed back around and past her into the fog at an easy pace. She walked back into the swamp, her wide hips swaying suggestively from side to side as they sank back beneath the surface of the water.

"Come with me."

The naiad's breath tickling the back of her neck a moment ago had made Sally go weak in the knees, and it took her a moment or two to fully process her sudden and casual approval of her request to stay and study for a time, but when she did, she let out a squeal of joy.

"Thank you, thank you, thank you!"

Before then remembering that she was *supposed* to be a noble and elegant representative of her order.

"Oh! Um, or rather…"

Reining in her exuberance, she bent forward once more in a formal bow as she said with as much dignity as she could muster.

"Thank you for your kindness, Mistress Modan. You honor me greatly with your, um… benevolence."

Then, with a skip in her step that was made all the more springy by the soft earth beneath her feet, the young mage danced off after the naiad's distractingly swaying hips, not sure where she was being led to, but eager to get there all the same.

Chapter 2

Learning Her Place

Modan didn't deign to turn around, or even seem to acknowledge Sally's thanks as she descended deeper into the warm, green water. In mere moments, it had risen up to envelop her hips, then her hair, before finally stopping just below her shoulders.

Sally on the other hand was already ankle deep into the murky soup before it dawned on her just where it was that she was running headfirst into. Skidding to a wet and sudden stop that ended with her flopping heavily down onto her bottom with a splash, she let out a yelp and a low moan before climbing shakily back to her feet, now soaked from head to toe.

"Oh, horsefeathers!" she cursed sharply, her tongue automatically jumping to the most coarse of oaths her mistresses ever allowed her to use without a thorough mouth soaping afterwards, slapping her palms against her waterlogged riding pants with a huff.

"Please wait just a moment, Mistress Modan!" she called out, her voice earnest and pleading, terrified that the nymph might actually leave her behind if she took too long. "I just need to, um… to get undressed."

The last few words came out softer and far less confident than the others had as it occurred to Sally that she'd have to strip down to her skin in front of the impressive woman she was trailing after in order to join her in the bog. She wasn't exactly a shy girl per se, but usually the only times outside of bathing in the communal bath halls that she'd ever been so brazenly disrobed in front of another person was when Mistress Alviren was disciplining her.

The memory of her former mistress's stern gaze and having to undress in front of her (to say nothing of everything that followed afterward) made Sally blush even more, but she knew that she had no choice in the matter if she wanted to follow after the nymph, and so she forced herself to steady her nerves as she tried to will the flush in her cheeks to go away before the other woman noticed.

At the sound of the girl's splashing and her pleas to wait, Modan decided to stop and turn around. Once again she was far enough into the fog that the details of her face were indistinct, but Sally had no problem hearing her low chuckle or the wry amusement in her voice as she asked, "Why do you humans insist on putting those ridiculous things on your bodies, anyway?"

The question caught Sally by surprise as she was hopping around from foot to foot in a desperate attempt to wriggle free of her soaked riding pants, which were now clinging to her like a second skin thanks to all of the water they'd managed to absorb, and she nearly toppled back into the mud as she tried to think of how best to answer it. She'd never really given the notion of clothing any serious thought before. Humans simply wore clothes, that was all there was to it, right?

Part of her, the impish part that tended to get her into trouble, wanted to say it was because it made getting spanked more exciting, but she clamped down on that impulse lest she give the naiad any ideas.

Although Sally was unable to pick out the details of her face or the upper half of her chest floating lazily just above the surface of the water, Modan had no such problems watching her, and seemed to rather enjoy the show the young mage was putting on as she struggled to free herself of her wet and muddy clothes.

"Hurry up now. I won't wait forever, you know."

Her admonition lit a fresh fire under Sally's rear end, and with a grunt she finally managed to free herself of her riding pants, small clothes, stockings, and boots all in one mighty push that sent them flying onto the shore of the lake, and which sent *her* tumbling head over heels into the shallow water with another loud splash and a heavy *thump* onto her now naked bottom. A moment later her journeyman's belt, tunic, and cloak went sailing through the mist after her other clothes, followed by her spectacles (which she wafted far more gently on a tendril of heated air).

Then, naked as the day she'd been born, she was back on her feet and sprinting noisily through the water just as fast as her feet could take her.

"Wait for me, Mistress, I'm coming!"

Modan continued to float in the water and watch as Sally's breasts and hair bounced and bobbed damply until they were swallowed up by the lake. Chest-deep for the naiad was almost neck-deep for the shorter girl, and with a quirked eyebrow Modan asked, "I trust you can swim?"

"Yes Mistress," nodded Sally eagerly as she eased up onto her tip toes to keep her head above water, grateful that she at least wouldn't embarrass herself by flailing around like a cat tossed into the wash basin. "We all learn in our first year at the monastery."

Her face felt warm from a heady mixture of being naked within arm's reach of the imposing and enticing woman, and from the heat of the water itself. All around her it was hot and steaming, but not scalding, and the tender caress of the liquid across her sore and aching muscles (and parts beyond that made her blush just thinking about) felt absolutely *wonderful*.

She was starting to see now why the water nymph always seemed to be smiling.

I could get used to this...

Seemingly satisfied, Modan nodded and moved onward into the water once again until only her head was visible above the surface. From there she glided backward, still not leaving a ripple, as she kept her eyes focused on Sally. She watched in amusement as the girl felt the water all around her growing warmer, its currents beginning to caress along the contours of her naked body.

"What is a monastery?"

Treading water and doing her best to keep her gaze focused on the endless fathoms of Modan's deep, black eyes instead of casting them lower in an attempt to probe the water's depths for a glimpse of her naked flesh, Sally smiled fondly to herself as memories of her life among her Celestine sisters bubbled up to the surface of her mind.

"It's like..."

She paused for a moment, groping for the best way to frame her explanation so that the nymph would be able to understand.

"It's a place where powerful older mages gather as many younger ones as they can in order to teach them all about how to use the Power. It's a wonderful place full of learning and all sorts of interesting books and things to see, and it's where I've spent the last nine years of my life studying under Mistress Alviren."

Upon uttering her mistress's name out loud, something that she hadn't done for many weeks now since leaving the monastery, a fresh blush that had nothing to do with the heat of the bog flooded Sally's face. Part of her really missed her former instructor and wished that she were back home in the monastery right then studying with her, but she knew that she was just being childish. She'd made the decision to set aside those feelings of homesickness at the start of her journey, and she wasn't going to let them creep in now.

She was a journeyman mage, and she would honor her mistress best by seeing as much of the world as she could and growing her powers, not pining for days gone by like some wide-eyed novice girl!

"Is it like a temple?"

Modan's question brought Sally back to reality and she nodded quickly, swallowing a mouthful of water in the process.

"Exactly!" she said with a cough, kicking her feet a little harder than she meant to and launching herself above the surface of the water so that her round breasts bounced free for a split second before sinking back down with a splash.

In her excitement at having been able to get Modan to understand what she was talking about (something that was a bit of a rare occurrence whenever she tried to explain things to others, if truth be told) she'd let herself get a little carried away. Blushing and smiling awkwardly in a silent apology for splashing around like she were back home swimming in the water woods for fun, she settled once more into a more dignified tread that befit her role of wandering mage.

"I see." Modan said, thoughtfully. "I used to have a temple, you know."

A moment of silence descended upon the two of them as they swam past several thick, mangrove-like trees and over to the edge of a round clearing. Above them was a break in the roof of branches and hanging creepers, and sunlight filtered down weakly through the column of steam. In the center of the lake, Sally saw now that there was a crescent shaped island lined with tall standing-stones, and in the center of that island she could just make out the edge of a pit of boiling mud.

"This is where I dwell," explained Modan, gesturing toward the central island.

"Wow…" breathed the young mage, completely overcome by the sheer, raw majesty of it all.

"Mind the water-snakes," added Modan, seemingly as an afterthought, amused by the girl's naked fascination. "They'll only bite if you provoke them, but I'd still be careful if I were you."

Sally's mostly-even swimming momentarily devolved into a graceless flailing at her warning about the snakes, her words immediately making her think that she felt something thick and slimy slithering past her under the water. Then, realizing that thrashing around in their home may count as provoking them, she forced herself to resume her rhythmic treading.

"R-right!"

With that, the nymph turned to fully face her, eying her coolly, her lips just above the murky, steaming water.

"So, what is it that you wish to learn?"

"Everything! I want to know everything there is to know about you, Modan," answered Sally in a rush, forgetting to include the title of "Mistress" in her excitement as she beamed brightly at the woman in front of her. "All the books in the monastery only ever mentioned water nymphs in passing with stupid stuff like, 'never cross a water nymph' or 'only a fool steps into a nymph's domain uninvited'!"

At these, she pitched her voice into a low mocking baritone as if quoting one of her dusty old instructors, before realizing that that probably wasn't proper behavior either and adding with a stiff bow of her head and a stutter.

"I-I mean… I just want to learn everything there is to

know about you. How you live, what you eat, how you spend your free time... You know, the basics."

"Hmmm... Well, you haven't crossed me, *yet*, and I did invite you, so I suppose you probably think that you have nothing to worry about?" pressed Modan, hovering just a foot away from the blonde acolyte, her lips ever so close to the young mage's as they twitched up into a predatory grin.

Sally felt her breath catch in her throat.

"Um... yes?"

At that distance she was able to make out the faint aquamarine hue of Modan's mouth and nostrils, and the wet, black pools that were her irises and pupils.

She has such beautiful lips... she thought before catching herself and blushing even more. *Stop it, Sally, you're here to learn!*

Modan merely giggled again at the girl's apprehension and replied, "Very well then, allow me to answer your silly questions."

Floating lazily in front of her, she shrugged.

"I simply... live. I eat minerals, dissolved nutrients from the volcanic mud and the sludge on the swamp floor, algae and seedlings in the water, little fish and shrimp, the occasional tadpole, flies and dragonflies, birds and snakes, and of course, fruit and dead animals."

Her eyes took on a hungry gleam, then.

"I don't *usually* eat things with my own mouth per se, but sometimes..."

"Sometimes...?" prompted Sally, completely spellbound.

With a secretive smile, Modan ignored her question and instead glided smoothly past her and over to one of the thick, winding roots that formed a ring around the inner pool that circled her central island and climbed up onto it, her big, dripping body almost luminous in the fog.

"Come. Join me over here."

As if she were a moth drawn to the light of her glowing body, Sally swam after the naiad, soon reaching the winding root and scrambling up onto it with far less grace than Modan had shown. Despite it having been a relatively short swim, she suddenly found herself short of breath as if she'd been swimming laps around the shallow lake for the last hour.

Modan sat on a little cushion of damp moss covering the root, and patted the spot beside her.

"All of this talk of food has actually made me crave a bite."

She then looked at Sally expectantly.

"Really?" asked a suddenly reinvigorated Sally as she eagerly scrambled over to sit beside her on the branch.

"Wow, a chance to see an actual water nymph *actually* feeding, how exciting!" she gushed, all thoughts of stoic propriety blown away in the face of learning something new.

"Well?" prompted Modan, raising a green-tinged eyebrow. "Let's see how well you understand the Power. Think carefully about where you are, and what you're doing, and then try to make food again."

Caught off guard by being thrust into another opportunity to impress the nymph, Sally straightened up in her mossy seat and closed her eyes. With a shudder, she brought her breathing back under control, taking in air through her nose in slow, steady streams before letting it out through her mouth as she sought the energies of the forest all around her.

She could sense Modan, her aura like a supernova among the stars of the plants and creatures around them, and it took her a few moments to adjust to her glare. But when she did, she was able to trace a line up the tree they were resting on and along a branch that hung just a few feet above them.

This time around she didn't let herself rush, instead slowly and methodically adjusting the structure of the tree branch until it began to bud with fresh apricots. However, try as she might to focus her thoughts and channel the Power, all she was able to do was make the branch tremble and bud.

Gritting her teeth, she redoubled her efforts until sweat began to bead across her brow, but again, she just couldn't do it.

Opening her eyes and looking shamefacedly down at her hands resting on her naked thighs, she let out a frustrated whimper and mumbled, "I can't…"

Modan gave her a stern, disappointed look, but there was still the hint of a smirk on her lips.

"What are these fruits you are trying to grow?"

"Apricots…" replied Sally, squirming under her gaze as she glared sullenly at the shriveled, half-formed buds of what were *supposed* to be delicious treats for her host. "I'm sorry, Mistress…"

Some mage she was. Modan wasn't about to let her stew in her own self-pity though.

"I have no idea what an 'apricot' is. And more to the point, neither does this tree. Have you seen any of these 'apricots' since you entered the forest? Or even outside of it? Perhaps where you come from, the trees have had all of your favorite sweets browbeaten into them, but these ones are *free*!" she scolded, leveling a haughty glare at her. "What kind of temple are you from, girl? It's been a while, but I still remember what would happen to cultists who had such presumption in the days when I was worshipped!"

Modan's sharp words, sounding more and more like her former Mistress Alviren with each passing moment, made Sally's bottom clench involuntarily as she whipped her head back up to petulantly glare at her before protesting in a voice that came out far more whiney than she meant for it to.

"I wasn't trying to *browbeat* them! I was just... I mean, the apricots back home are always so tasty and I just wanted to... I never meant to *hurt* your trees, Mistress. Honest, I swear it! I... I just wanted to share something that always made me happy with you is all..."

She wanted to ask what Modan meant by "in the days when I was worshipped," but that could wait until after her apology had been accepted!

Modan simply shook her head, her long, wet hair swishing back and forth around her. Truth be told, her memories of the old humans who once lived and worshipped within her domain were dim, but some things had managed to stay with her better than others, and the treatment of errant cult initiates was something that had always managed to tickle her.

Without a single moment of hesitation, she turned and wrapped both of her strong arms around the presumptuous little mage and hauled her over her ample lap, yanking her forward so that her wet, moss-flecked cheeks were raised above her warm thighs and her swaying breasts were pushed into the rough bark of the root beside her.

"Enough babbling!"

With that, she delivered five hard, sharp, elbow-powered slaps against the fullest part of Sally's lower cheeks, right where they looked to be the most sensitive.

SMACK! SMACK! SMACK! SMACK! SMACK!

"What are you-? Aieee!" cried Sally, her question transforming partway through into a squeal of surprise and then pain as a fiery sting exploded across her naked rear end.

Countless centuries of swimming (and maybe just a touch of the Power) seemed to have gifted Modan with a palm whose impact managed to send little bits of moss flying with each impact while making the spot where she'd just struck suddenly feel as if it had been smacked ten times in a row by Mistress Alviren's most wicked ebony hairbrush.

In short, it *hurt*!

All thoughts of propriety having now flown right out the window, Sally began to squirm and writhe over her punisher's broad lap, knowing full well that she couldn't escape, but still promising to be good anyway as she scissored her ankles back and forth behind her.

Long years of punishments in the monastery had taught her well.

SMACK! SMACK! SMACK!

"What is *wrong* with humans these years?" fumed Modan, keeping her slapping hard and fast, alternating between cheeks to make them wiggle and ripple. "They're either chasing the wolves, bragging about their pointy things, teasing the knuckers, or else making the poor cauldron trees grow 'apricots'!"

Still slapping non-stop, she used her other arm to yank Sally further forward across her lap so that she could spank her right on the dimply creases where her bottom swelled out from her thighs, raising her right arm even higher as she began slapping faster.

"Oh please- Ack! Mis- Oh! Mistress Modan- Owie, owie, owie! I'm sorry, I'm sorry!" cried Sally, her squeals and wriggling ratcheting up several notches in intensity as her poor, delicate sit-spots were roasted by the naiad's furious palm. "I'll grow you whatever you want me to, I promise! I didn't mean to upset your trees, I was just trying to help!"

Modan smiled haughtily at that as she shifted her aim back up and resumed spanking all over poor Sally's naked bottom, making each round cheek jiggle and bounce in one direction and then another as she painted their milky surface a vivid shade of bright red. As she continued her swatting, she shifted herself around under the crying girl in order to better feel her wet, naked skin against her own as her soft weight struggled and squirmed delightfully across her lap.

Oh yes, this was definitely the best way to deal with disrespectful humans.

Especially ones with such cute, chubby backsides.

"Yes, you will!" she chided, her voice carrying a distinct note of self-satisfaction to it as she tried to see how many swats she could dish out in the span of only a handful of seconds. "You are going to learn a great deal from me, little mage, and when you disappoint me, you… will… be… *punished*!"

Struck by a cruel bit of inspiration then, Modan decided to land the next twenty smacks right along the deep cleft between Sally's generous nates, intent on making the insides of her cheeks just as red and sore as their now-swollen centers and sit-spots.

The young mage's face blushed bright red and nearly as hot as her rear end as she felt Modan's slick fingers move to spread her bottom cheeks apart in order to gain access to her extra-sensitive inner cleft, exposing the creamy white skin there and her little puckered anus to the gentle caress of the bog's warm mist.

"Wait, no, Mistress. Not there, please!"

High-pitched peals of mortified agony soon rang out from deep within her as the naiad set to work painting streaks of blazing fire across one of the most delicate parts of her backside, just as she had with her sit spots. It was devastatingly humiliating, but in spite of that Sally found herself panting heavily while parting her thighs and arching her back in order to give her new mistress more direct access to her target.

After all, she was nothing if not helpful.

This of course all happened on a mostly subconscious level for her, as the girl's attention was focused more or less exclusively on trying to ride out her punishment and promising to be good from that point onward, wailing at the top of her lungs.

"I'll obey, Mistress, I'll obey! Whatever you wish of me I'll do it! Please, no more, I promise I'll do as you say and I won't *ever* disappoint you again! I'll practice every single day, I swear it!"

—

Modan on the other hand was content to just continue mercilessly punishing Sally, completely untouched by the buxom mage's cries, yelps, and struggles.

For one solid minute she focused her efforts entirely on delivering one brutal slap after another all around the lower thirds of the delicate tush trapped across her lap, determined to make sure it would remember this lesson every time it sat down for a very long time to come before letting her attention wander down to the shifting pair of thighs that she'd barely been paying attention to so far.

There was a lot of area to cover, and she was content to take her time and make sure it all got a *very* thorough going over.

After all, it was vital that this adorable human learn her place in the natural hierarchy of her swamp if she were ever to have any hope of understanding the things she planned on teaching her.

So she spanked.

And spanked.

And spanked.

Modan eventually stopped slapping Sally's cheeks when both of them were at last a uniform shade of cranberry red, and visibly puffy and swollen to the touch, as she'd started to grow bored of making the young mage yelp and squeal. She then relaxed her hold on the poor girl's back, and began to use her right hand to curiously knead and pet her buns, enjoying their radiating warmth.

It was comfy, almost like her hot spring home.

Throughout this post-spanking ordeal, Sally was left to pant and moan, thighs squirming together with increasing need as she lay across the lap of the powerful and commanding water nymph, sniffling into her makeshift moss cushion, and occasionally letting out little yelps whenever her strong hands found a spot that was particularly sore or ticklish.

Unfortunately for her, there were a lot of them.

"Hmmm… you know what?" chuckled the naiad, pulling the ruby red cheeks laying across her lap apart to inspect the clenching and unclenching entrance hidden between. "I think I could definitely get used to this."

Chapter 3

A Lesson in Manners

"Oooh, Mistress…" moaned Sally through a mournful sniffle, wriggling in place across Modan's knees as she caught her breath.

Now that her bottom was no longer being set ablaze, she was able to think straight again, and it began to dawn on her just how royally she'd screwed up. And with that realization came a fresh wave of panic.

"I am *so* sorry that I displeased you. I promise I'll do better from now on. Whatever you want me to do, I'll do it, I *swear*. I'll practice whatever you tell me to. I… I'll clean your swamp! Whatever it takes, just *please* don't make me leave before I've had a chance to learn from you!"

"Clean my swamp?" giggled Modan, her laughter rich and darkly musical as she gently rubbed Sally's bottom. "It's not dirty, but perhaps I'll have you clean it anyway… whatever that would entail. No one's ever offered to do that for me before."

Still chuckling, she reached out with her free hand to casually pet and play with the exhausted mage's golden hair. Pulling her silky locks free of their frazzled bun, she ran her fingers through them while with her other she began to slowly trace her forefinger down along the divide between the panting girl's cheeks, almost, but not quite, rubbing at what she found smoldering just at its base.

"Mmmm…" groaned Sally, eyes rolling up as her back arched on reflex. "M… Mistress, I…"

Modan leaned over her captive acolyte, deliberately squishing her large, wet breasts against her back, and then snatched something up from a nearby tree branch.

"Get up," she ordered, leaning back again and patting Sally's sore buns gently, but firmly.

The naiad's post-punishment ministrations had left her gasping and shivering in embarrassed delight, but she still scrambled to obey as her weight shifted off of her.

"As you say, Mistress!"

Kneeling awkwardly next to her on the mossy root, torn between sitting and kneeling (and wondering with some trepidation if not fully sitting down would result in more spanks), she slowly and reluctantly eased herself back onto her tender bottom and let out a low hiss. She would definitely be remembering this spanking for a long time to come, that was for sure. Modan spanked even harder than Mistress Alviren on her best days!

At least I have an entire bog's worth of hot water to sooth my poor bottom in...

Looking totally serene and composed, and perhaps maybe just a little bit smug, Modan reached out and offered her a handful of swollen, black berries.

"Here, these were already ripe."

Using her other hand, she popped one of them into her mouth and crushed it between her teeth, humming a little to herself and licking the dark, purple juice from her lips.

At first Sally eyed the unknown berries warily, but she quickly decided that if Modan was willing to eat them, then they were probably fine for humans too. And so, with a helpless shrug of her shoulders, she popped a couple of them into her mouth and bit down. Instantly, any wariness she might have been feeling vanished, washed away by the berries' sweet juices as they flowed along her tongue.

"Oh my."

With a massive grin, she popped four more of them into her mouth and chewed eagerly, savoring their unique flavor.

"These are delicious!" she declared happily around a mouthful of berry pulp, some of their juices dribbling down her chin from the corners of her mouth as she did so.

Then, suddenly remembering her manners, her burning bottom a vivid reminder of the times when she'd acted so unladylike back at the monastery, she hastily wiped the back of her hand across her mouth and blushed.

"Um… sorry," she mumbled, before popping another berry into her mouth with a bit more restraint, chewing it carefully before swallowing this time.

"Sorry, and…?" prompted Modan, raising an eyebrow expectantly.

"And…?" stalled Sally, making sure not to dribble any juices this time as she racked her brain for what the nymph was expecting her to say next. "And, um…"

Oh horsefeathers! she moaned silently to herself, drawing a blank and squirming uncomfortably on her mossy perch as the throbbing in her bottom grew suddenly more pronounced.

With no warning other than a cruel grin, Modan once again grabbed hold of her by the shoulders and hauled her right back over her lap and into the exact same position she'd been in just a few moments earlier, getting back to work delivering full-armed spanks to her already sore sit-spots.

SMACK! SMACK! SMACK!

"What about 'thank you'?"

This time she didn't bother with building up any steam, but instead just picked up right where she'd left off, delivering open-handed swats to the two bouncy cheeks stretched out across her thighs with the same speed and ferocity as she had at the very end of Sally's previous spanking.

"Ack! Oh! Owie!" squealed the already-sore mage in surprise, the fires in her bottom lit anew as her mind raced to catch up with the fact that she was back over the water nymph's lap getting spanked for being rude.

Shocked and appalled at her own lack of manners, and knowing full well that she deserved every single smack she was getting, she gritted her teeth and took her spanking with only the minimal amount of yelps and small wriggles for a full minute before finally breaking down and crying once again.

"I'm sorry, I'm sorry!" she squealed into the mist. "Thank you for the berries, Mistress Modan. They were delicious!"

"You're very welcome," replied Modan breezily, stopping to rest her palm comfortingly on the top chubs of Sally's tush, petting her naked, quivering back for a brief moment before redoubling her spanking efforts. "But you are going to be a *very* polite human from now on! Do you understand?"

SMACK-SMACK! SMACK-SMACK! SMACK-SMACK!

With that declaration she sacrificed some of the force of her swats in favor of rapid-fire speed as she began peppering the repentant mage's burning buns randomly.

Half a heartbeat later, Sally's squirming and squealing rose to unprecedented new heights as she writhed over the naiad's lap.

"Yes Mistress, whatever you say, Mistress!" she howled. "I promise to be the most polite mage you've ever seen. I'll never, ever, ever, *ever* forget to say please or thank you ever again, and I'll always, always, *always* show you whatever courtesies a nymph is owed!"

She wasn't really sure what those courtesies might be exactly, but at that moment she was prepared to do whatever it took to keep her bottom from *actually* being set on fire. Even for a Cindertouched, that wasn't an inviting prospect!

"Yes, I'm sure."

Ignoring Sally's pleas, Modan continued to relentlessly pummel her ample backside for the next few minutes, the screams and cries of a girl who never knew her bottom could hurt so much from just a hand spanking alone echoing off of the tree trunks before slowly dying amidst the steam and fog of the swamp.

—

It was the human's own fault, really.

If she didn't have such an enjoyably jiggly tush, then she wouldn't have had to spank it so much.

In the end, Modan finally stopped swatting only once Sally's face was as wet with tears and sweat as it was from condensation, and her bottom was so hot that she could actually *feel* the warmth radiating out from it from nearly two feet away.

It looked even rounder and plumper now, and was certainly more eye-catching in its new color.

"Hmmm… I've changed my mind," she declared suddenly after spending a few idle moments kneading the girl's battered cheeks with both hands and running her fingers up and down, heedless of whether it was soothing or hurting. "I think I'll keep you here for several days and nights… Perhaps longer."

She squeezed extra-hard with those last two words, digging her fingernails in roughly against the tender skin of the moaning mage's central divide.

"You're a sweet little human…"

Pulling the sizzling cheeks in her hands away from each other, she smiled hungrily down at what she saw exposed there.

"Ah!"

Modan bit her lip and chuckled under her breath at the girl's entertaining reaction before continuing.

"Albeit a *very* naughty one."

She let out a dramatically long and exasperated sounding breath as she continued admiring the contents of her lap.

Oh yes, she could definitely entertain herself with this captured prize for a while yet.

"But I will still be happy to teach you how to properly speak to the trees, and the insects, and the waters. And perhaps even some *other* things too… should you please me."

Letting her captive's cheeks go suddenly, smirking as she watched them wobble back into place, Modan moved on to petting and caressing Sally's back and shoulders, and straightening out the girl's sweat-soaked hair.

"Have the rest of the berries, if you want them."

She then slapped her bottom just hard enough to reignite the fire, and giggled again.

"T-thank you, Mistress…" replied Sally with a shuddering half-sniffle, half-moan.

—

A heady mixture of relief that her spanking was finally over (at least for the moment), excitement that Modan had decided to let her stay and was willing to teach her so much, and a fluttering sensation in her lower abdomen at how she'd phrased her plans as her having decided to "keep" her for several days (or more!) washed over her, filling her entire being until she felt like she might burst.

Grinning lazily, she heaved out a satisfied sigh and popped the few remaining berries into her mouth all at once, chewing contentedly.

She had no idea what was going to happen next, but she couldn't wait to find out.

"No one has ever called me 'Mistress' before," mused Modan as she watched her eat. "But I think I'm growing to like it."

She leaned over her again then, and Sally felt a tender kiss on her blazing, right sit-spot.

"Oh!"

As the nymph's soft blue lips came into contact with crimson skin, the mage girl let out a short gasp of surprise as an electric tingle intermixed itself with the twinge of pain from the contact, feeling her heartbeat accelerate as she recognized the sensation of an empowered signature – a magical, personalized symbol created and sustained by the Power - being affixed.

"There. Now nothing in this swamp will hurt you... unless I tell it to."

"Wow! Really?"

A giddy frisson overrode any exhaustion Sally might have still been feeling after Modan had finished affixing her mark, the seal on the extra-sensitive undercurve of her right cheek seeming to make it even *more* sensitive for a brief instant as a new kind of warmth pulsed pleasantly from where it had been applied.

"Yes really."

Squirming in delight across the naiad's lap, it took a supreme effort of will for her to fight down the urge to crane her neck back and see what the mark actually looked like.

There would be time enough for that later, she supposed.

Modan just giggled, and tickled the sensitized spot a little with her fingers, which made Sally squirm even harder.

"It seemed like the best spot for it."

SMACK!

She then slapped the spot in question, much harder than any reasonable person would think necessary.

"Up you get."

"Ah!"

A yelp of surprise escaped from Sally's lopsidedly-smiling lips at the sudden, sharp swat, and she was back on her knees in a flash, kneeling beside her new mistress on the mossy root. Grateful to have her tender tush out of the line of fire for the moment, she sheepishly rubbed at the spot on her right sit-spot where she could still feel the ethereal presence of Modan's seal humming lightly, and offered the naiad a watery and deeply humbled smile.

"Thank you… Mistress."

Mistress.

The word tasted differently on her tongue than it had just a moment earlier, but she found that it was far sweeter than any berry or apricot could ever be.

Modan smiled warmly back at her, her dark, liquid eyes gazing deep into her own bright green ones before nodding once.

"It's almost sundown. Do humans still sleep at night?"

Looking up beyond the semi-open canopy above her, Sally was startled to see that the once bright, cerulean sky of afternoon – or what could be seen of it through the omnipresent white fog - had given way to the crimson of evening.

"My goodness, I've been here for so long!" she marveled before realizing that her mistress had asked her a question and was still awaiting an answer.

Fidgeting slightly and blushing as she tried (and failed) to make herself meet the fathomless depths of Modan's inky black eyes, she hurriedly added.

"Y-yes Mistress, I… that is to say, *we*, still need to sleep every night."

For a brief moment she considered elaborating about things like pajamas, bedtimes, curfews, and sneaking around to stay up late and avoid them, but decided that that might not be the best topic of discussion to broach with her bottom still naked and throbbing from her last spanking.

"Alright then."

Drawing in closer, Modan smiled lazily down at her as she trailed a hand up from just above the young mage's smoldering crotch, across her smooth belly, and over her breasts, stopping just below her chin and oh so gently tipping her head back so that she was forced to meet her gaze.

"Still hungry?"

Sally couldn't help but feel as if small surges of Power were pulsing from the fingertips underneath her chin, and meeting her mistress's gaze, she smiled back at her as the irrational desire to say something sassy welled up within her.

Now that the spanking was over with (or at least, Sally hoped it was over with), she realized that her stomach was still growling.

"Yes Mistress," she chirped, her soft smile giving way to an impish grin. "We humans cannot survive on a handful of berries alone, you know."

"Alright then," replied Modan, seemingly unfazed by the younger girl's irreverent tone, her own smile broadening as she stood up on the slick branch.

As she turned around, presenting Sally with an *excellent* view of her bare thighs, pillowy buttocks, and swanlike back, she reached into a hollow in the tree trunk and pulled out a thick, struggling, black snake. She spent a moment or two stroking its head gently with a finger, and then just as casually, snapped its neck.

"You prefer to soften your meat before you eat it, do you not?"

Dropping the now dead snake onto the branch between them, Modan sat back down.

"Can you make fire?"

Sally's heart had leapt up into her throat upon realizing that there had been such a big and scary looking snake so close to her this whole time, and with a nervous half-laugh, she surreptitiously ran her fingertips along the ethereal seal on her right buttock.

"Um… Yes Mistress, I *can*, but um…"

Feeling the tips of her ears starting to heat up again, she cast a sidelong glance back over her shoulder, nodding toward her crimson backside. Conjuring heat might have been the first spell she was taught, once the Celestine Order had recognized her as a Cindertouched, but right at this moment…

"I'm not so sure I'll be able to, um… to really, uh… you know, *concentrate* on channeling the power right this second."

Blushing to the roots of her golden hair, she cast her eyes down to her firmly pressed-together thighs and mumbled.

"Um, sorry about that…"

"Distracted by a different fire, are we?"

Modan smirked, and then picking up the dead snake, she bit down into it, tearing away a sizable mouthful of raw meat and scaly hide, chewing it thoroughly. As her jaw worked, she let the blood from the creature trickle down onto the branch beneath them, which in turn caused the epiphytes growing there to shiver and writhe as more of the blue-black berries swelled up in tight bunches. She then wiped most of the blood off of her chin and grabbed a handful of the berries, squishing them into the open snake for her next bite before nodding toward the others.

"Help yourself."

Grimacing at the... *primal* way her mistress was eating their meal, Sally briefly considered looking for some dry twigs that she could use to build a fire the old fashioned way, but just as quickly shrugged off the idea; it was far too damp and foggy for that to ever work. So, a bit reluctantly, she decided to embrace the moment and take it as a small punishment for not being able to focus and channel the Power while she was... well, distracted. Besides, the whole reason why she'd left the monastery in the first place was so that she could experience new things outside its walls, right? And so, seizing the other end of the thick snake in both hands, she grimaced at it for a moment and then bit down with all her might.

And nearly gagged.

Still though, she forced herself to push past her initial revulsion, and soon enough her need for food overrode her delicate sensibilities, and she was sating herself on the raw flesh of the snake as if she were a native girl of the Western Wastes.

It really wasn't that bad once you got used to the texture, actually.

In fact, it was kind of fun!

Having the soft warmth of her mistress by her side certainly made the task far more enjoyable as well.

"Maybe you little mortal things are more adaptable than I thought," observed Modan with raised eyebrows, clearly impressed.

She then flashed her a bloody smile and the two of them fell into a companionable silence as they ate their dinner, their mouths almost touching before they finally came to a stop.

—

When Sally finally declared that she couldn't eat another bite, Modan tossed the rest of their snake up into the canopy. From above them came the sounds of a brief scuffle in the leaves as unseen creatures fought for the remains. This disturbance went completely ignored by the mistress of the bog however, who casually wiped most of the blood and juice from her mouth and chin with a satisfied smile while the steam and fog took care of the rest.

The air here is like a constant, gentle bath... realized Sally as she wiped her own mouth and saw that she was far cleaner than she should have been given how messy their meal was.

"Ready for sleep?" Modan asked.

With a weary nod and a somewhat-strained smile, doing her best to focus on whatever was coming next rather than what she'd just done to that poor snake, Sally replied, "Yes Mistress."

Then, frowning and casting an eye about to take in the swampy water all around them, the boiling mud in the center of the clearing, and the massive, arching roots that could be used as benches, she blushed and asked tentatively, "Um... where exactly am I supposed to sleep?"

Then, feeling a sudden twinge of worry pulse unpleasantly in her stomach, she added in a rush.

"I-I'm not going to have to leave you and return tomorrow, am I?"

"You won't," came Modan's simple reply.

It was neither a threat nor a promise, just a statement of fact. One that that she seemed completely certain about. She then helped Sally back up to her feet with one hand gently gripping each of her upper arms. Their breasts were so close now that they were almost touching, and with an enigmatic, little smile, she gently backed the sleepy mage toward the knobbly tree trunk directly behind her.

"I suppose I *could* let you breathe water and allow you to sleep where I do," she drawled before giving her head a small shake. "But I can only sustain that for so long…"

Suddenly, cool, damp, rubbery ropes began to creep their way around Sally's ankles and waist, the longer, thicker vines that hung between the tree branches above them slithering their way up and around her nubile young body while Modan held her firmly in place.

Distracted as she was by the prospect of actually being able to *breathe underwater*, Sally was blissfully unaware of what was happening to her until it was far too late. Panicking, she began to thrash around against the vines and her mistress's unyielding grip as she cried out.

"Noooo! What are you doing? Let me go, let me go! "

But Modan simply shook her head with an amused smirk and replied, "I said that you would stay with me, sweet mage, and that's *exactly* what you are going to do."

She then spent the next several moments highly entertained as she watched the vines encircle themselves around Sally's legs and each of her arms, before finally wrapping themselves snugly around her chest, squishing her ample breasts outward through two of the tight coils. Moans of embarrassment, and more than a little bit of pleasure (which in turn produced even more moans of embarrassment), were wrung from the blonde girl as she continued to struggle valiantly (but ultimately futilely) against the creeping vines.

"But… but… w-what… what are you doing?" she breathlessly gasped as she wriggled within their slithering grip, her thrashing taking on a distinctly more *squirmy* quality to it as the seconds ticked by and she found herself more and more ensnared. "L-let me go…" she panted half-heartedly.

Modan just shook her head, rolling her eyes in exasperation.

"That's quite enough struggling!"

She crooked a finger then, and the vines obediently responded by yanking Sally forward, forcing her to bend over at an almost perfect ninety-degree angle and holding her in place with her arms raised up to either side of her.

Ducking under the grasping creepers, she stepped casually behind the trussed-up mage.

"You asked for a place to sleep, and I'm giving you one. And I'll have you know that I do *not* appreciate your complaints."

"I wasn't *complaining*, I was just, um… just…"

Trailing off as she cast her gaze back over her shoulder, Sally watched in mounting dread as she saw another length of vine lower itself from a higher branch and wrap itself three times around Modan's strong forearm, leaving a short, whippy length for her to grip in her hand.

Oh dear…

As if reading her mind, the grimly grinning naiad swished her little whip back and forth through the air a couple of times, before hitting her other palm with it.

THWACK!

It landed with a stomach-churning impact, and Modan took a moment or two to savor the look of terror in the young acolyte's wide eyes and fluttering lips before lifting her forearm high to deliver the first blow to her naked right cheek.

THWACK!

It was just as well that Sally was so thoroughly restrained right then as Modan cracked her vine whip across her already sore bottom. Had she not been held in place by the slick vines, she would have most certainly broken position and danced around clutching her welted buttock for over a minute! That would have definitely earned her extras had Mistress Alviren been the one wielding the lash, and she had a sneaking suspicion that Mistress Modan would not have been any more lenient either.

So instead she tossed back her frazzled mane of bright blonde hair and let out a long, high-pitched squeal of pain followed immediately by a jumbled mess of promises to stop struggling, to sleep wherever her mistress desired her to, and great sweeping declarations of total and complete obedience from then on if only she would just stop. But even as she babbled out her pleas, she knew that they would not be heeded.

"You always promise that *after* I've started punishing you. Never before. I wonder why that is?" mused Modan as she **THWACKED!** the short length of vine down again, this time higher on Sally's right buttock, before landing another **THWACK!** vertically on the opposite cheek.

At her unspoken command the vines bent the babbling mage over even further, forcing her round, red bottom to stick straight up into the air for more licks at random.

THWACK-THWACK! THWACK-THWACK!

Left and right, up and down, from one angle and then another, soon twenty lines of pure balefire had been cut into her already burning seat, wringing from Sally an unending chorus of wailing moans of pain, embarrassment, and the Power help her, *pleasure* from deep within her very core.

When the vines had yanked her further forward, thrusting her bottom up and back for even more discipline at her mistress's hand, she'd abandoned all pretenses of offering up excuses and pleas entirely and had instead simply cried and cried as she took every stripe that the naiad decided to give her.

She'd been lashed before on a few rare occasions when

she'd been a novice back at the monastery, mostly whenever she'd done something to *really* displease one of her instructors, but those sessions had never been anything like what she was experiencing now. Each caress of the impromptu whip hurt like the blazes, but coming as they were from her mistress, Sally couldn't help but take them all with the meek and open heart of a learner wishing only to serve.

Although that did very little to stop her from yelping in pain with each line of pain etched across her ample backside.

THWACK-THWACK! THWACK-THWACK!

Then, just like that, the whipping had come to an end and Modan was there caressing her smoldering cheeks, tracing the lengths of the puffy, swollen welts crisscrossing them with her fingertips in smug self-satisfaction. And as she savored her handiwork, the young mage soon found herself purring and panting as the throbbing ache in her backside pulsed its way deeper and deeper inside of her, burrowing its way between her parted, trembling thighs and making her lightheaded as her clit hummed with pent-up need.

In that moment she would have promised to crack open the moon itself using the Power had her mistress commanded her to.

"Oh gods below," she panted, breathless as her mind and body swam with conflicting thoughts and emotions, the lingering pain in her backside near overwhelming as it warred with her need for release.

Modan was content to just let her new student cry for a bit however, still petting and soothing her flaming cheeks as she drank in her squirming and breathy moans.

"Here," she said sometime later, stooping down to gather up something from the root beneath their feet.

Her voice now had a playful charm to it as she crushed a

handful of the berries they'd been enjoying earlier and began to rub the thick, cool juice all over Sally's maroon cheeks.

"These will help with the burn."

Modan's fingers explored every mark, every handprint, every swell and dimple, turning Sally's limbs to jelly as she massaged the soothing juices into her scalded flesh. She even crushed a second handful of the fat berries and worked their pulpy juice along the insides of her cleft, spreading her battered cheeks wide and making her gasp and squirm anew as cooling relief washed over her twitching rosebud, before finally rubbing an extra-thick layer over her carmine sit-spots, which she lifted up away from the girl's thighs for that purpose.

"Although, they might not help for long," she chuckled as she finished up and had the vines pull her thoroughly spent student upright once again before petting her hair and chin from behind. "At this rate, you'll be getting yourself in trouble again before midday tomorrow."

She giggled.

"And probably again after that."

She then pressed her soft breasts and hard nipples to Sally's back and whispered tauntingly into her ear.

"And you're going to be here for *several* days and *several* nights. Maybe even longer…"

With those ominous words still ringing in her ears, Sally could only watch as Modan swan-dove into the water below, once again without leaving so much as a ripple to mark her passing. The vines then hauled the thoroughly restrained mage up off her feet, provoking a shocked meeping and twitching from her as they shifted her off the branch entirely. She quickly got used to the feeling of helplessness and weightlessness however as the vines carried her, and soon they lowered

her through the steam until she was hanging just a few feet above the warm water, surrounded on all sides by life and thick moisture.

Coming to a gentle stop, they continued to cradle her so that she was lying face up with her arms and legs splayed out to either side of her. And a moment later, another thick vine then snaked its way down from the canopy above and looped itself under her head, easing it up into a more comfortable position.

"Comfortable?" asked Modan a moment later, sticking her face up out of the water beside the dangling Sally with a wide grin.

Despite the fact that this was easily the most embarrassing position she'd ever been in, Sally couldn't help but admit - with a spectacular blush - that she was indeed quite cozy.

"Y-yes Mistress, I'm very comfortable…"

"Good."

Reaching up, Modan gave the acolyte's bottom one final squeeze from below, savoring its springy warmth.

"Sleep well, little human."

And with that, she disappeared soundlessly back into the murk.

Exhausted, Sally quickly followed suit and soon sank down after her new mistress into the world of dreams.

After all, it had been a *very* long day.

Chapter 4

Morning Refresher

Sally awoke slowly with the dawn of the next day, the warm caress of the mist rolling across the water and the low murmur of the creatures of the forest all around her gently coaxing her out of what had easily been one of the most refreshing night's sleep she'd had in a long time. The swirling eddies and currents of the Power hung just as heavily in the air of the bog as the mist did, and to a budding mage like her, it had been as if she'd been rocked to sleep while swaddled in the softest of down comforters.

With a long yawn, the young acolyte out on her first real adventure away from her monastery opened her bright green eyes to the soft morning light filtering in through the canopy overhead and tried to rub some of the sleepiness from them.

And of course, that was when she remembered just *how* it was that she'd been "prepared" for bed the night before.

Naked as the day she was born, she lay suspended just a few hand-spans above the calm waters of the bog's central clearing, her ankles and wrists wrapped snugly by vines that coiled up her arms and down her legs, spreading them lasciviously out to either side of her while still more cradled her around her waist and the back of her head. She wasn't particularly *uncomfortable* per se in her makeshift bed-harness, but any movement outside of fruitless wriggling was impossible for her at that moment.

Under any other circumstances, she would have been thrashing about in a frantic attempt to escape from such a humiliating snare, but these were hardly normal circumstances she found herself in. No, she had been suspended in this lewd snare by the mistress of this bog, Modan. She was her guest, and as embarrassing as they might have been, the vines wrapped around her were an embrace from her new mistress, not a trap that needed fleeing. Besides, she remembered all too well what had happened the night before when she'd tried to struggle out of the naiad's special "embrace", and the thought of it made her stomach do several flip-flops in a row as her thighs involuntarily squirmed toward each other.

The memory of the voluptuous and commanding water nymph mercilessly lashing her already well-spanked bottom with a whip fashioned from one of the thick, yet supple, vines from the canopy above while she stood trapped and bent over nearly in half by ropey tendrils that refused let her do much more than clench her cheeks and toss her hair about sent a fresh surge of heat rushing up Sally's face and a pleasant thrum along her exposed vulva, and it took a supreme effort of will on her part to rein in her racing thoughts before they could drag her away to the places she only dared to venture during those quiet moments when she lay in bed alone at night.

A sloshing sound from somewhere off to her left finally managed to fully yank her thoughts away from the memory of the way Modan's fingers had felt as they'd caressed her tender buttocks, and turning her head atop the vine loop supporting it, she saw one of the reptilian creatures from the day before splashing around near the shoreline. Wait, no, not one, but *two* of them! The large, hulking masses of teeth and hard, scaly muscle were plodding their way through a shallow patch between the gnarled roots of two massive trees, pushing their oversized faces through the mud and shallows.

Hmmm… They must be looking for food…

As Sally squirmed in her harness to get a better look at them, it suddenly dawned on her that a trapped (and pre-tenderized!) mage girl suspended just above the surface of the lake they were hunting in might just look like a *very* tempting breakfast to the pair of hungry knuckers.

Nothing to see here, just go about your business, please, she silently willed the two of them, holding her breath and doing her best to lie completely still.

As if reading her thoughts, the vines coiled around her suddenly constricted her soft flesh in a silent admonition not to be silly.

"Ah! Hey, watch it!" she yelped indignantly, squirming anew in their tightened clutches as her breasts were squeezed hard enough to make her wince. "I'm *trying* to be inconspicuous here. Humph!"

A few moments later the vines relaxed their grip again, and with a fresh surge of not unpleasant flip-flopping in her stomach, she allowed herself to go limp in their embrace as her mind flashed back to the empowered signature that Modan had placed on her right sit-spot the day before. The one that would keep the creatures of the bog from hurting her.

The one that marked the young mage as *hers*.

The two beasts on the edge of the lake continued tearing little fish and worms out of the mud for a while longer, growling and making other, stranger noises at each other as their faces drew closer. Eventually, one of them looked up and took notice of Sally, cocking its horned head slightly while making a strange, almost gurgling noise in the back of its throat. A moment later, a stream of red fire rushed forth from between its widely-spaced jaws, but it just as quickly dissipated leaving only a little smoke behind, and with a snort and shake of its massive body the creature turned back toward its mate. The two of them then sloshed back down into the water, disappearing beneath the surface with a few ripples and leaving her once again alone with only the singing of the birds and the bubbling of the hot spring in the distance for company.

"Wow…"

Remembering that the creatures wouldn't attack her had freed Sally up to observe them without any worries, and once she'd started, she found that she just couldn't take her eyes off of them! She'd never even *heard* of a knucker before yesterday, and she'd just now been given the opportunity to observe *two* of them in their natural habitat.

"Goodness me, how lucky can one girl get?"

The way they moved and fished with their huge scoop-like jaws, the way they interacted with each other, not to mention the way they could apparently conjure flames in their mouths like dragons, absolutely fascinated her. And once again she was overwhelmed with that same burning desire to know everything there was to know about Modan and her mystical bog that had drawn her there in the first place.

"Alright now, let's just see what else is going on here…"

Taking a deep breath to clear her mind, Sally closed her eyes and tapped into the swirling eddies of the Power flowing all around her. This time she didn't actively try to impose her will on any of the plants or creatures she touched (she'd learned that lesson the hard way the day before), but instead simply allowed herself to flow along the ethereal currents, observing, touching, sensing…

Perhaps it was her tranquil state of mind. Perhaps it was some arcane connection from the clinging vines. Perhaps it was just practice. But for whatever reason, this time when she opened herself to the unseen world she was able to see the greater pattern of the eldritch currents all around her in a way that up until then had always eluded her. All around her there existed a pulsating network of energy channels; rivers that carried the Power zigzagging back and forth through the water, into the canopy, and across the clearing.

Oh my... thought Sally to herself in awe. *It's... it's beautiful!*

At first this new window into the realm of the arcane was quite overwhelming for her, but after taking some time to adjust to her new way of seeing things, she was able to trace those flowing channels she discerned all around her back to their nexus. With a start, she saw clearly now that every line of Power within her perception eventually twisted and spooled its way back into the boiling mud of the central island, coiling around the standing-stones there and then descending deep into the burning pit at its center which glowed just as brightly as Modan herself had in the spirit world.

It was *incredible*!

Sally felt a giddy smile spread across her lips as the greater patterns that she'd heard her mistresses at the monastery talking about for so long *finally* came into focus for her. So accustomed had she been to touching the less distinct and unrefined energies of the Power, that for several long moments all she could do was stare in awed wonderment. Eventually though, focusing on the nexus point emanating from the deceptively small island became too overwhelming for her comparatively inexperienced mind to handle, and she had to pull away, retreating back to the less intense flows of the trees and the water around her instead.

At least those didn't threaten to consume her entirely if she wasn't careful.

"Good morning, Madam Tree," she greeted, calling out the venerable oak cradling her above the water, with a lazy yawn. "Thank you for holding me while I slept."

In response, the vines supporting Sally began to squeeze in a bit tighter. Not quite enough to cut off her circulation, but still definitely making things a lot less comfortable for her all of a sudden.

The unexpected constriction wrung a surprised squeal from the young acolyte and induced another round of squirming. The feeling wasn't exactly *painful* (at least not yet), but it certainly wasn't pleasant either, and was definitely more than a little jarring. Plus, seeing the coils wrapped around the generous swells of her breasts starting to dig deeper into her skin only served to make her blush and drive home just how naked, vulnerable, and exposed she was right then.

"Please, Mistress Modan already spanked me! I've already been punished. I'm sorry!"

Despite her heartfelt pleas and carefully restrained attempts to loosen the vines' grip on her body without actually crossing the line into actually trying to free herself from them lest she get into trouble again, the only reaction she got for her efforts was an almost vindictive constriction from the treacherous green ropes clinging to her.

She continued to struggle for several long and increasingly embarrassing minutes after that until finally she heard an amused voice from directly below her ask, "Now what did you say to those vines to upset them so?"

At the sound of the low, familiar voice coming from somewhere beneath her, Sally let out a squeak of surprise and relief. Squirming around as much as she could, she craned her head back to pout at Modan and in a panic-stricken voice cried out, "Mistress, help me, please! I didn't *do* anything. I was just trying to say thank you to this stupid tree for holding me while I slept and now it's trying to squeeze the life out of me!"

Modan just laughed.

"The trees aren't doing anything. Think a little harder."

She then reached up and ran a gentle hand lovingly, but

firmly, along Sally's back. Her fingers were slick with water after having just emerged from the lake and their passage along the groove of her spine tickled, but also served as a subtle reminder of what that hand was capable of.

Swallowing hard, Sally shivered and a fresh gasp that had nothing to do with the constricting vines clamping down on her escaped her lips. Taking a long, shaky breath, she did her best to try and puzzle out the meaning behind her words, and then with a sudden start she realized her mistake.

Feeling twin spots of color burst into life on her face at the novice blunder she'd been making that whole time, she did her best to once again re-center her mind as she focused on the *vines* holding her in place and cried out, "Madam Creepers, I am soooo sorry. I didn't mean to offend you, I *swear*! So please let me go, you're squeezing me much too tightly!"

In response, the vines immediately released Sally, falling away like cut ropes to dangle from the branches above and letting her drop unceremoniously into the warm, muddy water with a loud splash. Great flocks of birds immediately took flight as she landed, startled from their nests by the sudden noise, and Modan laughed merrily, clutching her sides and shaking with great gasps of delight.

A moment later the now soaking mage splashed up out of the lake, spluttering and spitting out a mouthful of silt as she kicked frantically and tried to get her bearings. Wiping great dollops of mud from her eyes and pushing back strands of waterlogged hair from her face, she glared up at the now placidly hanging vines and then leveled another pout at Modan. However, try as she might to be upset, she found herself smiling ruefully back at her almost immediately.

"Well, at least she let me go."

"It's a they, not a she," corrected Modan, still grinning mirthfully as she took hold of one of Sally's shoulders and wiped some of the dripping blonde hair out of her eyes. "The cauldron trees hate the arch vines for weighing down their branches and covering their lower leaves. They secrete poison to weaken them, and use sweet scents to attract insects to eat their clinging roots. The arch vines need the trees to survive, but they also fear and resent them because of this."

She stroked Sally's cheek with her thumb as she spoke, clearing away more silt and smirking at her.

"Appealing to the trees while in the vines' clutches? Rather insensitive of you, don't you think?"

Still grinning, Modan continued to float in front of the now mostly-presentable Sally and waited for her reaction.

"I wasn't trying to be rude!" she protested, waving her hands through the water in front of her as if she could somehow shoo away the misunderstanding between her and the plants.

"Rude people seldom mean to be." chided Modan, her face turning grim as she fixed the young mage with a hard look.

"I um..."

Feeling her cheeks flush with fresh heat while at the same time marveling at the hidden struggle that she'd been totally unaware of until just then, Sally tried her best to meet the inky black gaze of her mistress, but ended up staring at a lily in her hair just above her right ear instead.

"T-they aren't going to stay mad at me are they?"

Softening her features, Modan began gliding backward through the water toward the edge of the clearing, keeping her pace slow enough for Sally to keep up.

"Don't worry, the vines have thick skins," she reassured her, her lips quirking up at the corners. "But I'd avoid any clusters of them for the next few hours though, if I were you. They might just decide your bum's gotten a little too pale since last night."

"Right…"

Casting a wary glance up toward the green tendrils hanging innocently from the branches above her, Sally quickly started splashing after her mistress, doing her best to stay close in the hope that any creepers with designs toward swatting her would think twice with Modan close by.

"Wait for me, Mistress, I'm coming!"

Smirking to herself, Modan led the way over to a shallow sandbar of mud and roots between the trunks of two massive trees, not unlike the one Sally had seen the knuckers foraging on earlier, rising out of the knee-deep water with her usual non-ripple.

Hot on her heels, the young mage quickly joined her, sloshing through the thigh-high muck to stand in front of her, eagerly awaiting whatever lesson she had planned next but also feeling a sudden need to restore some of her credibility as a student.

"Ahem."

Clearing her throat, she straightened up to her full height, pulling her shoulders back to look the naiad straight in the eye and inadvertently thrusting her chest forward in the process.

"T-thank you for teaching me about the trees and vines, Mistress."

Modan nodded, accepting the thanks without comment.

"Tell me what you wish to learn about this morning."

She strode casually in front of the girl so that her large, curvaceous body was silhouetted in profile against the mist of the bog while she retained her mischievous little smile.

Sally noted that the flowers in her hair and skin were a little pinker that morning.

"Um…" she answered slowly, her mind suddenly feeling

like it was trapped in the mud sucking at her heels as her eyes traced over every curve of the naiad's slick form, noting every detail and the position of every flower for future reference.

Shaking her head in an effort to clear it and refocus, she ventured tentatively.

"That's a good question, Mistress, but I'm not really sure how to answer it."

She blushed and looked away as she continued.

"I thought I knew so much when I came to your bog yesterday, but now I feel like I'm a freshly-inducted novice at the monastery... There's just so much to learn that I don't even know where to begin!"

Modan smiled. Not exactly understandingly, but close enough.

"You already seem to know a fair bit about the Power itself, but not how it moves on its own," she said as she knelt down, bringing the murk up to her waist. "Let's have a look."

"Um... a look?" repeated Sally, tilting her head to one side in confusion and feeling an unpleasant twinge of embarrassment at not understanding what it was that she was supposed to be doing. "What do you mean, Mistress?"

In response, Modan stood back up suddenly and lumbered with surprising speed into the confused mage, wrapping an arm around her midsection and forcing her forward so that her other hand could *SMACK!* her bottom hard!

"When I kneel down and ask you to look at something..."
SMACK!

Modan spanked her again, this time on the other cheek.

"...it would behoove you to do the same and *look... at... what... I... am... showing... you!*"

Unrelenting, she kept alternating cheeks as she lectured, keeping Sally's arms pinned tight against her belly as her free hand arced down against her bouncing backside with the force of a hammer striking an anvil.

Surprised once again by just how strong her new mistress was – just because she *looked* like a human that sure didn't mean she was anywhere near as weak as one – Sally squirmed helplessly in her vice-like grip and yelped with each hard swat that landed against her unprotected bare bottom, her wet skin making them sting even more than usual as she swished her feet back and forth through the water behind her.

"Yes Mistress. I'm sorry, Mistress. I'll kneel wherever you want me to, Mistress!"

Half a minute and fifteen hard swats later, Modan let her go, dropping her unceremoniously back into the shallow water with a splash. Then, grinning toothily down at her, clearly not actually mad in the slightest, she planted her hands on her wide hips.

"Understand?"

Rubbing her stinging seat beneath the water for a moment, Sally leveled a pout at her mistress that just as clearly signaled that she understood she wasn't in trouble, before gingerly climbing back to her feet. She really did feel just a *little* bit badly for her misstep though, and as she stood before her, shifting her weight from foot to foot, she was secretly relieved that she'd gotten spanked for it.

Then, realizing that she'd been asked a question, and not wanting to provoke any more punishment just yet, she squeaked nervously and dropped back onto her knees in the murk with a splash.

"Yes, Mistress. It won't happen again, I promise!"

"I'm sure it won't."

Somehow that sounded less than genuine coming from Modan, but at the same time it also sounded like she wasn't too terribly bothered by the prospect either.

"Now then, tell me, oh wise wizard," she crooned, easing back into the murk herself without so much as a ripple. "Why is the Power in this place so strong and willful?"

Splashing her freshly-used right hand into the mud, she lifted a little handful of it out of the water and held it before her, letting it trickle out between her fingers.

"Why are these trees and vines so much more alive and awake than the ones you're used to?"

"Hmmm…" murmured Sally, rubbing her chin thoughtfully and eyeing the dribbling mud before casting a speculative glance around her at all of the other plants and unseen creatures surrounding her in the bog.

Determined to impress this time, she took her time in answering, weighing the problem out carefully in her mind before finally replying with the eager enthusiasm that tended to grip her whenever she thought she'd solved a riddle.

"It's because of you!" she exclaimed, pounding her right fist against her open left palm for emphasis. "You're a water nymph, and you're really old, so *you've* had a long time to learn how to channel the Power, right? Which means that all of the living things around you get to, um… absorb the, um… energy coming from you…?"

The last few words of her rapid-fire explanation started to trail off into an unsure question as her confidence in her reasoning started to dwindle.

"Um… right?"

"I'm flattered," was Modan's ironically dry reply, looking far less impressed than Sally had hoped she would. "But why do you think I am *here*, and not in some other swamp?"

"Huh…"

Horsefeathers! fretted an increasingly anxious Sally as she cast her eyes back down to the murky water in front of her, mulling over the naiad's question and searching its depths for any clues that she might have missed.

"Oh!"

Looking back up at Modan eagerly as a fresh idea hit her, she shifted in the mud and pointed back toward the bubbling island in the central clearing of the lake that was ringed by the roots of several cauldron trees.

"Is it because there's a big focus point of energy in this swamp?"

"*Now* you're starting to pay attention."

Modan clapped her wet hands, only a little sarcastically this time, as she went on to explain further.

"Everything has a spirit, or had one at some point. Most just aren't strong enough in the Power for you to see or touch. I am one of the exceptions, and it is because of the hot spring water, and the minerals that it carries up from my mother's cavern, that I dwell here."

Sally nodded thoughtfully at this explanation, smiling in satisfaction to herself now that she was starting to draw closer to the answer Modan was trying to lead her to. However, the more she thought about it, the more she felt a fit of giggles welling up inside of her, and she had to quickly bring a hand up to cover her mouth before any of them could escape. The mention of Modan's mother and her cavern had led the young mage to idly speculate about what a young Modan must have been like, and that thought had inevitably led to her imagining the naiad's mother (who she could only assume was as a slightly older, gray-haired version of her) spanking her.

The prospect of the strong and commanding water nymph being turned over a parental knee for a spanking was just so silly that she couldn't help but giggle.

"Something is funny?" prompted Modan, looming over her student with eyebrows arched and her lips pursed in disapproval.

"N-no Mistress!" Sally quickly reassured her, suppressing another fit of giggles even as an all too familiar flip-flopping sensation seized hold of her lower abdomen, forcing her to add in a rush. "I just, um… Something just swam past me and tickled my foot was all. Please, continue."

Modan's only reply to that was a look of utter condescension.

"Really!" shot back Sally with a quick nod and a frantic waving of her hands, digging herself even deeper into her fib despite knowing that she shouldn't.

In an attempt to deflect her mistress's attention, she gestured as nonchalantly as she could back toward the central island and its bubbling hot spring, asking in a fluttering voice, "S-so that muddy, bubbly water is coming from your mother's cavern?"

Even though she'd only asked the question to change the subject, the notion of meeting Modan's mother was rather intriguing, and she found herself adding excitedly, "Oh! Could we go see her if we wanted to?"

So preoccupied was Sally with attempting to sidestep answering her mistress's earlier question, that the vines descending from the canopy above her head went completely unnoticed until they'd looped themselves around her stomach and chest and had begun hoisting her up into the air.

"Wha-? Aieee!"

She had a pretty good idea of what was about to happen next, but despite the sudden swell of butterflies in her stomach that always preceded a punishment, she knew that she deserved what was coming to her and didn't struggle (too much) as the vines slithered down and around her arms and wrists, pulling them behind her back.

All the while this was happening, Modan stood off to the side, watching with a haughty smirk as the babbling mage was hoisted up just above the surface of the water. At her silent command the slithering creepers then dipped her forward so that she was angled toward the murk below with her bottom high in the air and her legs dangling freely behind her. She then strode imperiously around behind her, and gripping her lower back, started delivering the fastest flurry of swats she'd endured so far. All of them right on the centers of her two sit-spots.

SMACK-SMACK! SMACK-SMACK! SMACK-SMACK!

"Do… you… really… think… you… can… *lie*… to… me?"

Yelping and crying out with each and every furious smack to her upended behind, Sally struggled ineffectually against the vines pinning her arms behind her back as she scissored her ankles back and forth above the water, wriggling and squirming for all she was worth as a blazing heat exploded across her naked bottom.

"I'm sorry! I'm sorry! I'm sorry! I'm sorry!"

Still though, she couldn't help but be a little bit grateful that Modan was punishing her. Despite how much it hurt, she knew that she deserved it, and was relieved that she wouldn't have to deal with the worry and shame of trying to keep her lie going anymore.

But gods below did it *hurt*!

Curse this mouth of mine! she wailed silently to herself as she started to sniffle. *It always loved to rush ahead and get me into trouble back at the monastery, and it appears that mystical bogs work just as well for it too. Humph!*

Ignoring her pleas, Modan kept wailing away at Sally's

lower chubs, bringing back the pain from the previous night's lash marks and adding a fresh layer of heat to them.

SMACK!-SMACK! SMACK!-SMACK! SMACK-SMACK!

"Now *tell me*," she demanded, making the mage howl as she delivered several extra-hard swats to the backs of her frantically wriggling thighs. "What… is… so… *funny?*"

Sally in turn let out a long, low wail that had very little to do with the inferno blazing across her naked rump. Knowing full well that she would have to give in at some point, but stubbornly refusing to do so right away, she gritted her teeth and took in a dozen more swats before finally breaking down and blubbering in a rush.

"I'm sorry, I'm sorry! I was just- Ow! I was just thinking- Oh! About your- Ah! Ah! About your mother!"

Tossing her honey blonde hair from side to side, she let out another high-pitched squeal.

"Owie, owie, owie! I'm sorry, I'm sorry! I just- Aieee! I just couldn't help- Ack! picturing her- Ah! Spanking you!"

Unprepared for that response, Modan stopped abruptly.

Then giggled.

And then started laughing absolutely uproariously.

"That's… that's…!" she howled, bending forward and clutching at her stomach as her entire body shook with great, heaving gasps of delight.

"Well, no… No, she never punished me," she finally managed to get out a while later, straightening back up and wiping away several tears from her big, wet eyes. "And I'll be happy to tell you more about her if you wish, but first…"

Gliding back around to face Sally, she reached out and casually snapped a long, whippy switch off of a low-hanging branch.

"Last night, you made a solemn vow that you would not

defy me again."

With a thin, cruel smile, she tipped the panting girl's head back with the stick in her hand, forcing her to look her in the eye as she continued.

"And you just now knowingly lied to me, didn't you?"

Sally felt the cautious optimism that had been steadily building up inside of her ever since Modan had stopped spanking drain out all at once, along with most of the color in her face, as she sagged in the vines' grip.

Oh dear…

Feeling an electric tingle arc its way down the curve of her spine to nestle itself between her aching thighs, she started to squirm again as the switch in her mistress's hand tickled her beneath her chin.

"I um… I-I wasn't defying you, mistress!" she stuttered nervously, the irony of defiantly protesting how she hadn't been defying her going totally unappreciated in her current state of panic. "P-please, I'm sorry! It won't happen again!"

"Hmmm… Those words sound hauntingly familiar," mused Modan with a toothy grin, tapping the switch lightly underneath the girl's quivering chin, "Perhaps the *next* time I hear them, they will be sincere."

She then sauntered back behind the mage, and at her silent command the vines let her torso dip further forward toward the water, elevating her already bright red bottom up even higher into the air.

*Whistle- **SNAP!***

A thick line as white hot and cutting as the vine whip's had been the night before then seared itself horizontally across the middle of both her cheeks.

*Whistle- **SNAP!** Whistle- **SNAP!***

A moment later, two more diagonal lines crisscrossed their

way across both cheeks as well, branding them with a bar and an X as if Sally were a particularly naughty bit of livestock.

"Ooooh, Mistress!" she howled as Modan etched her design across her arched backside.

In that moment she found herself wishing very much that she was better at channeling the Power while under duress. Maybe then she could have weakened that evil branch and made it snap.

"I *do* mean it, I dooo! Whatever you say, I'll do it. I'm not *trying* to be bad, honest, I'm not! Please forgive me!"

In response to her pleading, Modan added another, lower, bar to her thighs. And then an X to go with it.

*Whistle- **SNAP!** Whistle- **SNAP!** Whistle- **SNAP!***

"Gods below, I'm sorryyyy!"

She then casually tossed her switch aside and took half a step back to admire the now very elaborately decorated pair of cheeks swinging back and forth in front of her, waiting patiently for their owner to recover a bit.

Now thoroughly chastised and once again fully determined, even if not exactly confident, that she'd *never* give her mistress another reason to punish her ever again, Sally let herself sag in her restraints with a relieved sigh. Then, after managing to regain her composure enough to speak without a hiccup or a sniffle getting in the way, she looked back over her shoulder with a pair of watery eyes of her own and mumbled apologetically.

"T-thank you for disciplining me, Mistress…"

They were the words that Mistress Alviren had always liked to hear her say after she'd finished punishing her, and by the gods she meant them!

She's so incredible…

Even in her drained and weary state, Sally still couldn't

help but be mystified by her new mistress. Modan's presence, her easy confidence and mastery over the Power and all that dwelled within her domain, the sight of her looking back at her with a satisfied smirk on her face. It was all so overwhelming, and in that moment she wanted nothing more than to be just like her!

"You're very welcome, little human," answered Modan as she glided forward in the water and began to gently knead Sally's tender tush, seeming to relish the pained gasps her touch produced in her.

A few moments later the vines shifted the well-spanked girl back down onto her feet, and Modan wrapped her arms around her, holding her close from behind.

At first Sally stiffened in surprise, but then melted like butter in the naiad's strong arms. The embrace pressed her blazing backside in against Modan's thighs, and squished her large breasts into her back as she softly massaged her body, and it felt absolutely *wonderful*.

"Besides," giggled Modan, breathing her words softly against Sally's ear as she continued hugging her from behind. "I'm sure I'll be doing it again before long."

She continued to cuddle and pet her contrite student for a little while longer, Sally's sizzling buttocks pressed against her damp thighs, and her hands idly exploring the mage's curves, before slowly letting her go with a promise of, "If you're a good girl for the rest of our lesson, I may just decide to rub some more berry pulp on that."

She indicated the "that" she was referring to with a little slap on Sally's welted backside before continuing, making the girl yelp and stumble forward into the shallows, almost falling over.

"Now then, the hot spring water and minerals are filled with the Power. But what do you think happens after it flows up into this lake?"

Perking up at the mention of another rub down with those wonderful berry juices, especially given the way the crisscrossing welts on her behind seemed to be pulsing in time with the rhythm of her heartbeat, Sally vowed silently to be a model student for the duration of her lesson. Turning to face Modan, she could feel the corners of her mouth perking up. This time she was ready with an answer.

"It all gets sucked up by the roots of the plants and absorbed by the creatures that drink from the lake."

She slapped her fist into her palm again, practically dancing from foot to foot with the joy that came from unlocking another mystery of the Power.

"And *that's* why all of the creatures and plants around here are so lively!"

Modan smiled, much more warmly this time.

"That's exactly right. It seems your temple isn't as bad as I had feared."

She gestured up at the tall trunks and their roof of branches and vines.

"The trees drink the water and swallow the minerals for hundreds of summers and winters. And all that time, the Power grows within them. However, they can expend but a little of it on their own, unless prompted by a quicker mind."

She paused again and looked expectantly at Sally.

"But what else can happen to that Power?"

"Um…" she replied, drawing the word out as she looked around at the trees of the bog in the hope that one of them might shed some light on a clue.

Gods and goblins! What else could there possibly be? she asked herself in mild exasperation. *Aren't vines that hold you in place while you're getting spanked and trees that get offended at their neighbors enough already?*

"Oh!"

With a start, Sally realized that she'd been staring off into space mulling the problem over and that Modan was still waiting on her for an answer.

Unfortunately she didn't have any.

Oh well, better be honest, I suppose... she thought with a rueful rub of her tush.

"I'm sorry, Mistress, I don't know what to say."

Modan just shook her head.

"And here I was starting to get my hopes up..."

Kneeling down, she fished a wriggling shrimp from out of the murk and cupped it in a muddy hand.

"The Power sleeps in the plants and fungi. They think too slowly and too dreamily, to use it for anything but growth and health unless another force acts upon them."

Standing back up again, she held the little crustacean out in front of her.

"But animals eat the plants, and everything within them is passed on to the animal. Drinking the water of this bog empowers them. But eating the plants that have been drinking that water and storing that Power for so long? That provides a *much* greater increase."

Suiting actions to words, she popped the muddy, wriggling thing into her mouth and chewed it absently.

Sally grimaced at the crunching noises she heard coming from the dying crustacean, but quickly remembered that she was her mistress's guest, and as such was *supposed* to be a noble and elegant representative of her monastery, and so managed to catch herself before she could make any faces that might offend her host.

"Those animals are in turn eaten by other animals, and

they inherit all the Power of their prey, each of which retains most of what it took from the green things."

As if on cue, there came a mighty splash and then a horned, scaly head with three beady red eyes erupted from the water just a few feet ahead.

"Ah!"

The knucker glared at Sally with its glassy, reptilian eyes and growled a little bit before climbing up onto the shallows and shaking its head dry. It then opened its mouth, and with a low growl, crimson flames began to light up between its jaws.

"And of course, the oldest and most vicious predators are the ones who have the most Power."

"I…"

Sally swallowed hard, doing her best to maintain her composure.

"I see…"

The explanation made a lot of sense, and the sudden appearance of the knucker and its mouth full of fire was more than enough to dispel any lingering doubts that she might have had.

Doing her best to keep a quaver out of her voice while also at the same time slowly inching around in the mud so that Modan was standing between her and the beast, she eased up onto her tiptoes to look at it over her shoulder in wonderment.

"Is that why you're so strong, Mistress? Because you're so old and you've been eating the things in this bog for so long?"

With an excited gasp, she added.

"Could *I* become as strong as you are if I ate more of them?"

She eyed the knucker speculatively, wondering just how she'd ever be able to make one of them her evening meal, before deciding with a shiver that she'd most likely have to make due with eating mounds of shrimp and gross tree snakes instead.

"Oh, humans…" chuckled Modan with a shake of her damp black hair. "Always so obsessed with power."

"What? I'm not *obsessed*," huffed Sally.

"Yes, I'm sure."

Still smiling, the naiad leaned over and gave the girl's bottom another slap, just to make her jump.

"Ah!"

"But to answer your question: No. Ingesting the water and its essence helps to keep me healthy, but it does not empower me."

Turning away from the knucker (which was now probing around in the mud with its snout in search of a snack), Modan leveled a look of matter-of-fact confidence at her student.

"I'm just a part of it."

"Oh, I see…" repeated Sally, mostly not lying as she tried to puzzle out just how someone could literally be *part* of the Power.

It was a concept she'd never really given much thought to before. Of course she'd seen it mentioned in passing here and there in some of the books in the monastery archives, but she'd always just assumed that the authors were over exaggerating or being poetic.

Now she wasn't so sure.

She had a feeling that this was something that she'd be puzzling out for a long time yet to come. That it wasn't something she was *supposed* to fully grasp right away.

She loved problems like that!

Plus mulling over the idea of Power being made manifest in a sentient, physical form helped to distract her from her mistress's earlier chiding. Although she knew that the naiad had mostly just been joking with her about being power-hungry, the rebuke had still hit just a little too close to home for her liking and she found herself muttering grumpily under her breath as she idly traced her fingertips over the raised edges of one of her welts.

"I am *not* obsessed with power. I just don't want to be a terrible mage is all…"

Apparently though, Modan had far better hearing than she gave her credit for.

"Don't want to be terrible?" she queried, pulling Sally away from her self-conscious musings as she glided without a ripple across the muddy sandbar toward another cluster of tangled roots, sinking down to her waist as she entered the little hollow beneath them. "What risk is there of this?"

Sally felt the spots of color in her cheeks intensify at Modan's question. She hadn't actually intended for her to hear her mumbling about her insecurities! In an effort to cover up her embarrassment, she scrambled off after her, making more than enough splashes for the both of them. Still though, the question wasn't one she'd been expecting to be asked and she found herself replying without much thought.

"Risk? What do you mean, Mistress?"

"You said you don't want to be terrible. What makes you think you are, or will be?" elaborated Modan, turning around and beckoning Sally down into the watery hollow after her. "I've been called terrible before, you know. It wasn't so bad. I actually kind of liked it."

She chuckled.

"Although, 'Mistress' certainly has a charm all its own."

Modan's candor lifted the young mage's spirits, and before she could stop herself, she was pouring out her deepest fears to her in a rush.

"I just… I just want to be a *proper* mage!" she exclaimed with an exasperated sigh, emphasizing the word "proper" with a frustrated splash even though she wasn't really sure what she meant by it yet. "I study and I study and I *feel* like I'm learning, but then I get around great and powerful ones like you and Mistress Alviren and I turn into a floundering mess who can barely answer your questions. And then to make things worse, I always somehow end up doing or saying something silly that lands me over your knee getting spanked!"

Feeling her stomach twisting with the familiar anxiety that she was walking a knife's edge, half a moment away from being dismissed and sent on her way (although if she'd ever stopped to think about it she'd realize that had never actually happened), she added hurriedly.

"I'm trying my best, Mistress Modan. Really, I am!"

Modan just shrugged and beckoned her closer.

"I don't know anything about this Alviren you prattle on about, but you seem to be learning."

"You really think so?"

"I have no reason to lie."

Beaming brightly at the plainspoken praise, Sally scrambled into the hollow and threw herself at Modan, wrapping her arms around her in a tight embrace and gushing, "Oh thank you, Mistress!"

It then dawned on her that clinging to an ancient and powerful water nymph without her permission probably wasn't the most elegant or refined of actions one could take, and she made as if to untangle herself from around her water-slicked body with a blush.

"I mean… Um… Th-thanks," she mumbled with much

more restraint as she tried to ease back to a more respectful distance, keeping her gaze locked on the point over the naiad's stomach where a belly button would have been on a human.

I guess a nymph wouldn't have one... she mused to herself, more as a way to ignore her embarrassment than from any actual academic curiosity.

But Modan didn't let her pull away.

"There's still more for you to see," she declared firmly.

Pulling the mage in tight against her taller, thicker body, half-in and half-out of the lukewarm water and holding her close so that their wet forms were pressed firmly against each other, she gave her next order.

"Close your eyes."

Letting out a small contented sigh, the heat from her mistress's slick body radiating into her like the warmth of a bonfire on a cold winter's night, Sally did as she was told and waited patiently for her next command.

—

Modan grinned, enjoying the feel of the dreamy-faced girl in her arms as they stood there surrounded by fog and mist. Had she ever seen one so bright and beautiful, in this particular way? Modan's memories became cloudy more than a few years' past, and everything from the old temple that once stood over the bog was more a collection of disconnected images and sensations than anything else. She was sure, however, that if she had met humans quite like Sally Vinebrook before, there could not have been more than one or two of them.

She then raised a hand to the back of the girl's head, getting a firm grip through the tangled mess of blonde hair there, and angled her face up just a little higher. She watched in amusement as a shiver of surprise rippled through Sally, but the young acolyte dutifully kept her eyes closed even as her lips flickered in surprise. As Modan knew she would.

"Good girl," Modan purred.

After watching the girl's quivering face for another moment and giving her handful of hair a light squeeze, Modan leaned in. Bending forward to put their faces level, she placed her smiling lips against her student's trembling ones, sucking gently and letting her tongue explore the human's lips and teeth.

—

It took a supreme effort of will on Sally's part to keep her eyes closed and not flail her arms in surprise when she felt her mistress's aquamarine hued mouth come into contact with her own, but she quickly found herself melting into the moment.

"Mmmm…" she murmured, unable to stop herself.

As they kissed, she felt an electric tingle in her mouth that spread inward to her chest and head, and she let out a low moan of pleasure from the back of her throat as her knees grew weak beneath her. Thankfully though the naiad had a firm anchor to hold her upright with in the form of her hair, and she refused to let her go as their tongues intertwined and her body was filled with rippling, tingling waves of electricity that were even more exhilarating than channeling the Power.

It was incredible!

A minute later Modan finally pulled away, still lightly gripping her student's damp hair and holding her body against her own.

"Open them," she commanded.

Slowly, savoring every moment and sensation, Sally did as she was instructed. She could still feel a distinct electrical tingling inside of her mouth and nostrils, as well as a deeper thrum inside her throat and chest. The sensation was not unlike that of the feeling she'd had when she'd first received the sigil on her right sit-spot the day before, and she had to fight hard not to swoon just then.

Smiling up at Modan dreamily, her bright green eyes gazing deeply into the water nymph's inky black ones, she sighed.

"Mistress…"

"Yes?"

Blinking in surprise, Sally felt the tips of her ears heat up with embarrassment.

She hadn't realized she'd spoken out loud.

It hadn't been a question or a statement, just a reaction. An outward manifestation of all the thoughts, feelings, and sensations bubbling up inside of her like some new potion she was brewing for the first time.

"N-nothing," she mumbled, looking chagrinned before adding. "I just… Um… thank you."

"You're welcome."

Modan fondled Sally's back and hair for a moment longer, and then looked down at her eyes and mouth lovingly before releasing her completely.

"Follow me, now. It won't last forever."

With that, she turned and descended into the hollow, flooded root cave, her head vanishing beneath the muddy, steamy water without so much as a ripple to mark its passing.

Chapter 5

The World Beneath the Murk

Sally stared after the retreating form of Modan's perfectly round, naked buttocks for several long moments before it suddenly dawned on her just what the tingling sensation in her chest must mean.

"Water breathing!" she gasped in delight, reaching up and feeling around her mouth and neck to see if there were any physical changes there. There weren't any as far as she could tell, but that did nothing to quell her excitement. With a huge grin plastered across her face, she ran off after her mistress, splashing and sloshing her way through the water until she too was totally submerged.

Out of habit, she held her breath and kept her eyes squeezed tightly shut as her head dipped below the surface, and it took her mind several moments to convince her body that it was still okay to continue breathing. She managed to get the hang of it soon enough however, and upon cautiously cracking one eye open she was startled to find that not only was she able to breathe without a problem, but she was also able to see with crystal clear clarity through the swirling murk as well.

With a skip in her step that was dampened only slightly by being underwater, she sloshed her way forward to Modan's side, beaming as she gurgled in delight.

"This is *amazing* Mistress!"

Modan just smiled, patting her shoulder and nodding her head. Submerged as she was beneath the water, her dark hair now floated around her like a black halo and her breasts lifted up in the buoyant environment, lending an even more ethereal quality to her already mildly luminescent form.

"Come."

Gesturing ahead of them, she half-walked and half-swam forward under the tree. Its roots held open the mouth of a tunnel lined on all sides by winding, twisting tendrils of wood, just barely holding back a heavy wall of mud and silt. The tunnel itself was far from dark however. All around its walls and along its ceiling, brightly glowing worms wriggled their way in and out of the muddy cracks between protruding roots, bathing the gloom in a soft, multi-hued phosphorescence as small, soft-shelled crabs scuttled past their ankles and deeper into the tree-cave.

"Gods below…" Sally half-gurgled and half-gasped in astonishment, her eyes growing wide as saucers as she was led through the opening. Unable to stop herself, she repeated again, "This is amazing!"

Never in a thousand lifetimes would she have ever thought that such a strange and wondrous place existed just beneath the deceptively placid waters of her mistress's bog. Although, now that she gave it some thought, she supposed that she probably shouldn't be *that* surprised either. She'd been routinely having her preconceived notions about the world around her challenged ever since she'd arrived, after all. Still though, the unknown territory stretching out before her was absolutely fascinating! Even here she could feel the gentle warmth of the Power pulsing out in steady waves from the small crabs and the even smaller worms squirming and scuttling around them. It was all so new, all so foreign, all so… *beautiful.*

Seemingly on a whim, Modan stooped forward and plucked up one of the glowing, multicolored worms from the mud. She then took hold of Sally's right hand and wrapped it around her third finger like a ring.

"What is it, Mistress?" she breathed quietly, feeling her heart skip a beat as she stared transfixed at the coiled creature for several long moments.

She made sure to do her best to keep her hand as still as she possibly could, scared of accidentally startling the little worm into trying to escape, and held her breath for good measure, watching to see if it would move. However it soon grew apparent that it wasn't going anywhere anytime soon. If anything, it seemed to have frozen into place, unmoving, but still glowing softly.

"Just a pretty thing," answered Modan with a shrug, her deeply melodious voice sounding somewhat muffled beneath the water.

Still smiling, she once again resumed leading the way further down through the tunnel, guiding them into a little cavern where several other tunnels all converged. There she took hold of Sally's wrist once again, and raising it up high enough to cast the rainbow glow of the worm on her finger over the gloom, revealed in its center a great pit filled with silt and soft organic material, upon which sat a massive ball of legs, antennae, and chitin.

"Oh my!"

Sally let out another gasp of surprise that came out as a stream of bubbles from her mouth, and she had to immediately clamp down on the urge to retreat back behind her mistress at the sight of the creature before her.

Her first impression of the… thing… was that of a giant insect, then a crab, and then finally a lobster's segmented body with many eyes and huge, oddly-shaped claws. The creature was bloated and soft-bodied except for where hard plates dotted its surface, and was at least as large as she was. As she watched, it seized one of the soft-shelled crabs still scuttling along the muddy floor and guided it up into its mouthparts, chewing heavily.

"W-what is it?" she asked with a mixture of awe and just a *little* bit of worry as she watched the massive, unnamed creature enjoy its meal.

It just had so many… appendages…

"An old charax," answered Modan, gliding smoothly around the edge of its lair and motioning for Sally to follow.

Which she did.

Very slowly.

The charax didn't seem to take much notice of her presence though, or if it did, it was plain that it didn't particularly care that she was there, and soon enough she was once more standing at her mistress's side.

As she sidled close, Modan gestured up to the cavern ceiling, where a few large, unusually thick tree roots had punched through to hang down above the creature's pit. As they watched, the charax took the broken, mostly-empty shell of the crab it had just been gnawing on and placed it on one of the roots, which in turn began to very slowly curl around it. The charax then looked back down the tunnel where they'd come from, and a moment later another crab scuttled from it and marched straight into its pit. The charax grabbed it, and just like the last one, brought it up to its mouthparts and began eating.

Scooping up a pinch of mud between her fingers, Modan held it in front of Sally, then pointed to the glowing worm around her finger lighting the cavern, then at the crab, and then finally at the charax.

"Do you understand?"

Very slowly and deliberately, Sally moved her gaze from

the mud, to the worm, the crab, the charax, and then finally, the tree, puzzling out what she was supposed to be learning. Then, all at once, it came to her, and she beamed.

"Yes!" she exclaimed, beginning to tick off points on her fingers. "The worms consume the mud which is saturated with the Power. The crabs then eat the worms absorbing that Power. After which the charax eats the crabs, and then in turn *it* feeds the trees!"

She clapped her hands and eagerly rubbed her palms together, dancing from foot to foot in the soft earth, positively bubbling with excitement.

"It all trickles upward from creature to creature!"

Modan smiled and nodded.

"Correct. But it is also much more than that."

Gesturing back toward the mouth of the tunnel they'd just emerged from, she went on.

"You see, the worms bore the life from the tree roots. The crabs rid the trees of them, and the charax then returns some of what was lost back to the trees... eventually."

She then pointed to the woody, muddy wall behind Sally.

There she could see hundreds and hundreds of hollow bits of crab legs jammed into it in neat rows.

"Every spring when they wake from their long sleep, the trees consume the remnants of the crabs left to them by the charax, thereby restoring a measure of the Power that was lost to them by the worms."

Sally stared in wide-eyed fascination at the wall of legs only a few hand-spans in front of her, mouth agape and filling with swirling silt as she tried to wrap her mind around just how vast and complicated the ecosystem of the seemingly placid and sleepy bog really was.

"This is... This is *amazing*, Mistress..." she breathed

reverently, before her excitement overcame her once more. "Oh my, I have *so* many notes to make!"

"Indeed."

Nodding again and smiling ever so slightly in self-satisfaction, Modan gestured again and began to lead them out through one of the other tunnels as the old charax nonchalantly continued to enjoy its seemingly endless meal behind them.

"Most charax never grow to be that large," she explained as they swam forward. "When they are young, they sneak up on crabs and fish and other little animals, and are forced to hide from the bigger ones. However if they manage to live to sleep for five hundred winters, like the one you just saw, they grow to be great in Power... and in wisdom. The oldest charax can enchant their prey to happily feed themselves to them, and they are also able to ward the knuckers that once hunted them from entering their burrows. Their wisdom teaches them that the trees are important, and so they help them."

"Incredible..."

Sally swam slowly after Modan, still trying to take it all in. She idly wondered just what other nuggets of wisdom a strange crab creature who sat around all day eating smaller crabs might have, but for the moment her mistress's explanation made a lot of sense, and she tucked it away in the back of her mind for further analysis later on.

Up ahead of them she soon saw more light, and a moment later they exited the tunnel, emerging back into the central lake. Below them, Sally could see more of the crabs from the tunnel, as well as fish and fat water snakes, crawling about and mingling in their intricate waltz above the smooth stones lining the lakebed.

Hmmm... wait a moment now, she thought to herself

as something caught her eye, feeling only slightly ridicu-lous as she paused to float in the water and rub her chin contemplatively.

There were a great many stones covering the lake bed, many of them half-buried by mud. And while that on its own wasn't all that notable, there was something about what she was seeing as a *whole* that stuck out to her as odd. Staring harder, she soon saw that many of them were stacked on top of one another, almost as if…

No, not just stones! she realized with a jolt of excitement as a familiar series of shapes began to resolve in front of her in the murk.

That was a wall!

Now that she knew what to look for, it was clear to her that many, even most, of the stones in the lakebed had been deliberately stacked in a cyclopean fashion, though much of it had by now been worn away by centuries of water and nearly completely covered in tree roots. Nearly, but not entirely. It was obvious to the young mage now that she was looking at the side of a *very* old, and totally forgotten, building. And just beside it was the faint outline of a path. And a bit further on still, was that… a pillar?

This must have been where her cultists worshipped her long ago… Oh my, how fascinating!

Truly this was indeed a wondrous place.

"And this is just one bog!" Sally gurgle-squealed to herself in delight as Modan returned to the surface ahead of her.

Perhaps one day she could discover more. If her mistress had a mother, then it stood to reason that she also had sisters, right?

Kicking her legs in glee as her imagination began to con-coct vivid fantasies of forgotten relics and hidden temples full of mysterious creatures, Sally swam up after her guide, and as her head crested the surface, she couldn't help but giggle and beam.

This was all so *exciting*!

Modan was already there waiting for Sally with an indulgent smile when she at last broke the surface of the lake, floating a foot or so ahead of her and just high enough for the very tops of her round breasts to be visible above the waterline.

"How's your tush?"

Caught up as she had been in the whirlwind of her mistress's enchanted kiss and the revelation of the unseen marvels hidden just beneath the seemingly innocuous surface of her bog, Sally had nearly forgotten all about her earlier thrashing. However it seemed as though the crisscrossing patchwork of welts covering her bottom and thighs had just been waiting for Modan to call out to them, for no sooner had she mentioned them, then they began to tingle and throb once more.

Biting back on a wince and clamping down on the urge to reach back and rub at the tender ridges, Sally put on a brave face. She didn't want to seem ungrateful or petulant in the face of everything that she'd just been taught, after all, and so with a grimace that did little to hide her true feelings on the matter she replied.

"Um… It's fine Mistress."

Modan smirked.

"I thought you might say that. The minerals here are good for your skin. And excellent, we won't need any more berries for you, then."

Sally felt the brave face that she was putting on falter just a bit at hearing that – even as she made a mental note to try and collect some of the murky water to study more in-depth later – as she realized that she'd just fibbed her way out of having more of those wonderful berry juices applied to her tender nates. For a brief moment she considered revising that assessment of her rear end, but just as quickly dismissed the idea. She couldn't very well change her story now. That would just earn her *more* spanks for lying!

Turning away from her grimacing student, Modan casually glided back over to the edge of the central clearing and climbed up onto some roots.

Roots which Sally couldn't help but notice had intertwined themselves over the years across the tops of several suspiciously geometrically shaped stones.

"Although, I'm sure you're hungry, are you not?"

"Oh!"

Startled out of her self-pitying reverie, the young mage swallowed her chagrin and chided herself for being so silly as she swam over to join her mistress on the branch. What was done was done.

Besides, she *was* rather hungry.

"Yes Mistress."

"Heh. I thought you might be," answered Modan, grinning mischievously as she held up a struggling crab in each hand.

Her grin took on a decidedly more predatory bend to it then as she winked.

"I didn't think the old charax would mind."

Settling down onto the mossy top-cover of the branch, she gestured toward the spot next to her with one of the crabs.

"Come, sit."

Sally eyed the wriggling crab with another grimace, wishing very much that it was a piping hot meat pie or something sweet instead, before setting aside her longing and easing herself carefully down onto the (mostly) soft and moss-covered surface of the root-branch with only a faint wince. As unappetizing as the offering may have looked, food was food. And besides, if a powerful water nymph like Modan thought it was what they should eat, who was she to second guess? Still though, she couldn't help but wonder.

"Are they tasty, Mistress?" she asked while eying the crabs skeptically.

Maybe with a pinch of dragon pepper and a honey glaze...

Sally's stomach grumbled.

Living day to day on travel rations had definitely taken a toll on her taste buds, and the mere thought of eating something other than cured meat and stale bread was enough to make her mouth water.

"What? Humans don't eat crabs anymore?" asked Modan, looking a little ruffled, as if annoyed that humans would have the audacity to change their dietary habits over the course of centuries.

Sally blushed at the question, and accepting the squirming crab with a sheepish grin replied, "Um... Some people still do, I think. Around fishing wharves and near the ocean, I suppose. We usually just ate mutton or chicken at the monastery, though."

Determined to impress this time, and doing her best to ignore the way the uneven, rough grooves of the tree bark was digging into her tender hindquarters, she closed her eyes and cupped her hands around the crab, focusing her mind on summoning energy from the Power. A moment later there came a bright flash and a hollow *pop*, and it was instantly flash-fried in her hands.

Sally's face lit up with delight as the savory scent of sizzling crustacean meat wafted up to tickle her nostrils.

Success!

Mostly...

"Oh, oh, oh!" she hissed, juggling the suddenly *very* hot shell from hand to hand as she blew on it to help it cool.

Okay, so *maybe* the crab was just a *bit* crispier than she'd intended it to be, and perhaps it was smoking a little more than was probably healthy, but it was still cooked, and that was all that mattered as far as she was concerned.

"Impressive, little human." observed Modan with just a hint of amusement as she dug into her own crab.

"Why thank you, Mistress."

Feeling more than a little satisfied with her semi-clumsy handiwork, and grateful that she wouldn't have to eat another meal of raw meat, Sally sank her teeth into the hot flesh of her soft-shelled crab and ripped out a huge bite.

It was delicious.

"Hmmm… I think I remember chickens," mused Modan thoughtfully between slurps of raw meat that she sucked out from the broken exoskeleton of the still weakly struggling creature in her hands. "They had them here sometimes. I have never seen a 'mutton', though."

At that, Sally snorted, spraying bits of burnt crab and crumbled shell down her front in the process. Wiping away some of the debris from her face and chest with the back of her free hand, she turned to face the nymph and giggled (all worries about being formal and respectful overridden in that moment by her mirth) as she explained, "Mutton isn't a *creature*, silly. It's the meat that comes from sheep!"

Sally looked thoughtful for a moment then, staring off into space and idly tapping one slightly greasy forefinger against the side of her cheek.

"…Although to be fair, I don't really know *why* they call it that. It doesn't really make sense now that I think about it…" she added as an afterthought as she brought her hand back down to her lap and let her eyes wander over the various flowers blooming in the naiad's hair.

"Oh."

Modan just shrugged and took another slurp of her meal, the poor crab in her hands finally dying.

"And what's a sheep?"

"You don't know what a *sheep* is?" demanded Sally incredulously, finding it hard to believe that there was something she knew that her mistress didn't.

Modan narrowed her eyes then, and her tone grew suddenly frosty.

"Excuse me, but *you* didn't know what a knucker was until yesterday. Or a charax for that matter."

Setting aside her mostly-eaten crab, she narrowed her eyes.

"Um, Mistress, no, I wasn't... That is to say..."

She hadn't changed her position at all, but somehow she now seemed to be looming over the young mage, a frustrated predator regarding her tiresome prey.

"I only chided you for your ignorance of the Power because you claimed to be a priestess, and a scholar of it. By what right do you *dare* mock me?"

Suddenly entire swarms of butterflies were performing aerial acrobatics inside of Sally's stomach, and it was all she could do not to scoot away from Modan or jump off of their log to hide in the water.

"M-Mistress, I... I didn't mean to offend you!" she stuttered out nervously, her own crab forgotten beside her as she waved her hands in front of her in a doomed attempt to somehow snatch back the last few minutes. "I was just... It was just... I mean, I've never met someone who didn't know what a *sheep* was before. I didn't mean to imply that...!"

One by one, excuse after excuse started tumbling out of her

with increasing speed as she frantically tried to come up with something to say that would make up for her rudeness and quell the naiad's growing ire. Unfortunately for her, try as she might, that appeared to be a task beyond mortal ability now.=

Oh horsefeathers! she cursed silently. *You really know how to put your foot in your mouth, don't you, Sally?*

Modan in turn simply kept her wayward student pinned in place with a steely, narrow-eyed glare as she piled up her flimsy excuses and attempts to backpedal, until finally, she'd had enough.

"Stand up."

The words were spoken firmly and calmly, but they immediately cut through Sally's rambling.

"But-!"

With a throaty little moan that expressed just how scrambled and nervous she was feeling far better than any words could have, she reluctantly slid off of the branch and back into the shallow water to stand nervously fidgeting in front of her displeased mistress.

Still just looking at her, but somehow seeming to be looming over her from on high, Modan spoke again.

"Come here."

Sally's heart felt like a humming bird trapped inside her chest then, demanding that she run away, but she just couldn't bring herself to disobey.

"Y-yes Mistress…"

Swallowing hard, she carefully picked her way across the mossy mud and bits of branch, closing the distance to Modan's right side.

SMACK!

The irate naiad slapped her thigh, sending a sharp report echoing across the still lake and making her ample lap wobble and bounce, just as her student's already-welted bottom was about to.

"Bend over."

Again, the words were spoken calmly, but the sheer weight of authority behind them opened up a pit in the bottom of Sally's stomach, and before she could stop herself she was pleading again as she shifted nervously from foot to foot in the mud.

"Pleeease Mistress, I'm sorry!"

She knew it wouldn't work. That resisting would most likely just make things worse for her. But the sight of her mistress expectantly waiting for her to bend over was a frightening one, and she just couldn't help herself.

Modan was unyielding in her resolve however, and she kept her pupil's bright green eyes locked in the bottomless depths of her own liquid gaze.

"You do not want me to have to *make* you, little human."

Now that definitely made poor Sally's knees wobble, and with a frantic squeak she half-dove and half-collapsed in a heap across her mistress's waiting lap, all pretense at resistance collapsing in an instant as her well-appointed backside squirmed into place.

"No, Mistress, you're right, Mistress. I'm sorry, I'll be good!"

Modan just shook her head as a half-smile played across her lips at that, hungrily eying the delicious pair of cheeks being presented to her.

"I'm honestly not sure if you will *ever* be good at this point."

Still smirking, she gave Sally's arched backside an affectionate squeeze that made the girl gasp, wince, and shiver all at once.

"But I think that this will at least help make you better for a *little* while."

With that she leaned in hard against the naked girl's back and began another bare, wet-bottomed spanking, just like the ones from the previous day, only far worse due to the layered stripes and half-healed marks already there.

SMACK! SMACK! SMACK!

Just as before, Modan's hand was a ten ton boulder and her arm an avalanche as she brought it up to her shoulder before bringing it crashing back down to deliver a full force slap with her open palm straight against the softest curves of the wiggling and jiggling bottom laid out before her.

She didn't bother with lecturing Sally this time. The girl already knew why and how she deserved this punishment. Instead she simply focused on delivering a hard, fast, and absolutely agonizing spanking in the fog.

"Ah! Ack! Owie!"

Likewise, Sally didn't bother with launching into her usual chorus of promises to be good and proclamations of regret, instead clinging to her mistress's damp thigh as best she could and simply taking her spanking with squeals and cries that quickly dissolved into sobs.

As her spanking dragged on however, she began to feel a small twinge of worry rising up in the back of her mind. That twinge soon burst into a full on explosion of anxious panic as her endurance was pushed to its limit and then shattered entirely as Modan continued to mercilessly punish her bottom and thighs, all the while showing no sign of slowing down anytime soon.

SMACK! SMACK! SMACK!

Gods below and demons above! If this is a spanking that's supposed to help me behave for just a "little while", there's

no way I ever want to find out what would make me behave even longer! Sally thought to herself as her legs scissored back and forth through the air behind her in time with a flurry of particularly unpleasant swats along the inner curves of her sit-spots. *At the rate she's going, I'll be an old lady, withered and with my hair turned to gray, before I so much as even consider being naughty ever again!*

With a look of utterly serene focus and determination etched into her regal features, Modan kept up the pace of her swatting, not altering her speed or technique in the slightest; just hitting Sally's disobedient bottom, over and over and over again, the fleshy thwacks of her palm and the thrashing girl's anguished cries mingling together and drowning out the usually placid background noises of the bog. With a relentlessly cruel sense of determination, she methodically turned the young mage's entire bottom a very angry shade of bright, *bright* red, and then covered it all over again with another layer of hard smacks just to be thorough.

The entire ordeal only lasted a handful of minutes before Modan finally ceased her swatting, but to poor Sally it felt more like an eternity, leaving her panting and lying limp across her broad lap by the time it was all finally over.

—

"Mmmm...."

Feeling a keen sense of a job well done, the smugly self-satisfied naiad leaned forward and rested her elbows on top of the sobbing girl's sweat-sheened back, propping her chin on her palms and gazing haughtily down at her beaten flesh like a queen looking down from her throne.

And truth be told, it was quite the sight to behold.

Sally's already wide and well-endowed cheeks had swollen

considerably under Modan's careful attentions, and had taken on the color of fresh raspberries – like the ones she occasionally saw hanging from the bushes just outside her bog. With each shuddering breath the girl took they heaved hypnotically up and down, jiggling with each exhalation and wobbling above a matching set of equally-red upper thighs as well.

Modan licked her lips.

She looked absolutely delicious.

Chapter 6

Burning Backsides and Berries

It took several long minutes before Sally was finally able to catch her breath enough to stop sobbing and dribbling tears into the murk below her. By then the inferno in her backside had reached its zenith, and now began subsiding into only a lingering smolder, the coals beneath the surface of her tender cheeks radiating an almost pleasant warmth that throbbed in time with her heartbeat. It wasn't unbearable, just hot enough to leave her squirming and sniffling and wishing desperately that she could reach back and attempt to rub away some of the sting. Unfortunately for her though, she wasn't in a position to be able to do that just yet, but on the bright side, the weight and feel of Modan's soft, slick skin under her and her large, firm breasts resting atop her back more than made up for it.

With a watery sigh and one last sniffle, the journeyman mage let the last of the remaining tension in her body drain out, all but melting across her mistress's lap and sighing with a mixture of relief and contentment. As much as her bottom hurt, in that moment there was absolutely no other place she would have rather been. Especially since the throbbing ache in her cheeks was starting to work its way deeper and deeper between her shifting thighs now that she wasn't lost in a sea of tears and pain.

"Oh ho, maybe I can set fires after all?" giggled Modan as she pinched the reddest part of Sally's *very* red cheeks.

"Ah!"

Sally in turn hissed and squirmed in place across her lap, and in that moment it wasn't too far of a stretch for her to believe that perhaps her bottom might just have been set on fire at some point.

At least there's water nearby, just in case…

"Get up, dear."

Modan smirked and gave her ruby cheeks one last swat.

SLAP!

"You still need to finish your crab."

With a wince and a low moan that threatened to break down into more sniffles if she wasn't careful, Sally slowly pushed her way up off of her mistress's lap, using her leg and shoulder for support, before sliding back onto her feet in the water and surreptitiously dipping her sizzling rear end into the (comparatively) cool murk.

It didn't help very much, but it was still better than nothing.

Then, with another wince she eyed the rough, moss-covered bark of the root-branch that Modan was sitting on, and weighed her options. She was in no mood to sit on her battered bottom just yet, and so picking the lesser of two evils, she climbed back up onto it with a grunt and knelt awkwardly beside her mistress. It wasn't exactly comfortable per se, but it was still at least better than the alternative.

By some miracle of fate, Sally's charbroiled crab was still right where she'd left it before she'd gone over Modan's lap, and with a grimace she leaned over and snatched it back up. Then, shifting her weight from one knee to the other in a fruitless attempt to get comfortable, she slowly began to nibble down the rest of it, picking her way around the extra-crispy parts and sucking the softer meat out from the shell like she'd seen her mistress do earlier. She wasn't all that hungry anymore, but there was absolutely no way she *wasn't* going to finish eating her midday meal after she'd just been ordered to!

Watching her student nibble at her food, Modan was seized upon by a stroke of cruel inspiration.

"You look so uncomfortable kneeling like that," she crooned, her eyes twinkling with derisive mirth. "Sit down."

Sally moaned again and looked over at her pleadingly for as long as she dared to, hoping against hope that the naiad would change her mind, but not willing to risk going back over her knee again by pushing the point too hard. Modan just fixed her with her steely "do as I say" look however, and she knew that there was no escape from obedience now. And so, closing her eyes and doing her best to mentally prepare herself, squeezing her thighs together and squirming in dread of what she knew was going to be a very unpleasant sensation, she shifted her calves out from under her and eased herself with a pout slowly back down onto the mossy root.

"Ooooh…"

As her full weight came to rest atop the knobbly and ridged bark, she let out a low hiss that quickly devolved into a prolonged whine as the rough and uneven surface dug in pitilessly against her hot and swollen flesh, fanning the coals in her tush and reigniting the fire that Modan had stoked there only a few minutes earlier.

Oh horsefeathers and dragon spit, this stings! she wailed silently to herself, squeezing her thighs together even tighter and doing her best to ignore the warm, tingly sensations that this fresh pain was causing to pulse along her wet lips and aching clit. *I'm never going to be rude again for as long as I live, I swear it!*

Modan on the other hand was wearing the widest, cruelest grin that Sally had seen on her so far as she reclined back languidly against the tree trunk, eyeing the young mage hungrily as she stretched her legs out toward her.

"Go on, finish your meal," she ordered with a dismissive wave of one pale and lustrous hand. "But don't eat *too* quickly now. After all, that's bad manners."

"Humph!"

Sally fixed the crab in her hands with the poutiest pout she could possibly muster, and briefly considered retorting with something about how toying with people was bad manners as well, but clamped down on that impulse just as quickly as it presented itself. The thought of being rude to her mistress right now, even in jest, was enough to send a shiver down her spine and make her bottom clench involuntarily, and the twinges of pain that *that* elicited were more than enough to dissuade her from risking any further punishment for the time being.

So instead she chewed. It was slow work, and the rough bark biting into her battered buns only served to make it all the slower as she continued to shift her weight around in an attempt to find some position that *didn't* sting and hurt.

Unfortunately for her, there were none.

Eventually though, the last bite of her crab was thoroughly chewed and swallowed, and her meal was complete.

"A-all done Mistress…"

She turned to level a shaky smile at Modan, eager to show that she'd learned her lesson while doing her best to keep her wincing to a minimum.

"Good girl."

Leaning in toward her student now, Modan brought her knees up to her chest and rested her hands and chin on them.

"So, would you like some of those berries now?"

"Oh yes, *please*, Mistress!" gasped Sally, all but sagging in relief as she shifted to look more directly at her mistress, suddenly wishing very much that there was a lap there she could dive across to escape the torment of her stupid root-seat.

"Alright," answered Modan with a shrug, climbing gracefully back to her feet and giving the girl a complete view of her body, face, hair, and blossoms in the steam. "Use what you've learned so far, and bring me some. I'll be waiting here."

She smiled then, planting her hands confidently on her hips, deep dark eyes twinkling with silent laughter.

"I trust you're suitably motivated?"

A strangled cry of exasperation escaped from Sally's lips, but even if she wasn't able to have the naiad rub in those soothing berries right away, she jumped (literally) at the chance to escape from her awful perch!

This as it turned out, was a mistake.

She hadn't realized that while she'd been eating, that the rough bark of the root had slowly been embedding itself deeper and deeper into her soft and tender flesh. Her sudden jump to her feet had yanked it free all at once, which in turn had touched off a fresh blast of white hot agony that exploded across her bottom, causing her to yelp in pained surprise as her hands flew back to clutch at her swollen seat, knocking her off balance and sending her toppling head over heels into the water with a mighty splash.

Modan just laughed as she watched her student splash and splutter, clutching at her sides and wiping away a tear of mirth from her eye.

"Take your time, if you wish. I'm in no hurry, I can assure you."

Blushing to the roots of her sodden, honey blonde tresses, and now more determined than ever to find those berries, Sally gave another pouty huff and sloshed off in the direction of the cauldron tree that she and Modan had been sitting in the day before when she'd first been spanked by the naiad and taught about their soothing effects. She found the tree easily enough, but the berries growing nearby posed a bit of an issue.

There was more than one kind!

"Oh horsefeathers and dragon spit!" she cursed, feeling a panicked vice tighten around her heart as she stomped her foot in the muddy shallows with a *ker-splush* that sent water splashing in all directions. "What color were they again?"

Sally could see red berries, black berries, and even some dark purple berries. But which were the ones that Modan had used last time? Deciding that it was better to be safe than sorry, the throbbing burn in her backside making her extra-excited to be back across her mistress's lap post-haste, she quickly snatched up as many handfuls of each type that she could find, wrapped them in a big leaf, and then carefully paddled her way back to where the naiad was waiting for her, watching her progress with naked amusement.

"Here you go, Mistress!" she declared, eagerly thrusting her offering of the small mound of berries she'd collected toward Modan. "I couldn't remember which were the ones you used yesterday, so I just grabbed a little bit of everything I could find instead."

Still standing atop the log, Modan raised one eyebrow and dipped her chin down in mild annoyance.

"And how is that supposed to show me what you've learned?"

"Well, I uh…" hemmed Sally in reply, going pink in the face all over again as she stared down at her pile of berries and frowned. "I um… I was, um… I was hoping that maybe you'd show me which were the correct ones?"

Modan rolled her eyes at that and seemed to think about something for a long moment before finally settling down again, this time straddling the branch with her thighs on either side. In her new position, the black hair and faintly aquamarine lips between her legs lay openly exposed and presented to the young mage, but she didn't seem to even register this as she spoke.

"Very well, hand those to me."

"R-right!"

Relieved that she wasn't being sent back out to search again, and feeling her throat grow suddenly dry at the tantalizing sight so brazenly on display before her, Sally stepped a bit closer and passed the berries to her mistress. Nearly fumbling them into the lake in the process.

Modan accepted them all without a word, depositing the big handfuls into a small hollow that Sally hadn't noticed earlier, before bringing her legs a little closer together to form a suitable perch.

"Over my lap."

She patted her thighs again, though this time not particularly hard, as a mischievous, rather than stern, look stole across her regal features.

Sally was immensely grateful to have something else to do other than stare just then, and the mischievous look on her mistress's face coupled with those three magic words made her stomach flip-flop with delightfully nervous anticipation. Smiling shyly, she approached the naiad on wobbly knees and hoisted herself up awkwardly into position across her waiting lap, the new position of her straddling the log making the entire experience even more new and exciting as she settled in.

"Ready, Mistress," she squeaked happily, giving her bottom a little wiggle to emphasize her point.

"So I see."

Modan chuckled at the girl's cute enthusiasm, seeming almost surprised that she had the audacity to actually wiggle that swollen, ruby red thing at her after what she'd just done to it. With Sally's head and arms hanging over one side of the branch now, and her juicy thighs dangling down the other, her bottom was by far the highest and most visible part of her right then.

"Ahem."

Modan made a show of clearing her throat before plucking up a round, red berry, – not too unlike Sally's own swollen seat – and popping it into her mouth, chewing contentedly.

"The great honeyberry creeper gnaws its roots into the cauldron trees and sucks out their life, just like the worms you saw below. This is the source of its healing properties," she lectured, tracing a single fingertip idly across the taut, yet jiggly, surface stretched out before her. "The others you picked typically send their rootlings into mud filled cracks on the smaller islands, hang them into the rich water from tree roots or floating masses, or else catch insects with sweet-smelling traps."

Sally squirmed as the naiad's fingertip tickled her tush, and nodded her head eagerly, absorbing the knowledge like a sponge. She absolutely loved learning all about the different vines and the berries they produced, and this time around she did her best to try and commit everything that she was being told to memory. They all sounded so *fascinating*, and she made a mental note to examine them more closely later on when she had the chance.

"You know how to speak to the trees and herbs, and are capable of asking them which is which. So you *should* have remembered the aura and Power of the honeyberry, but you did not, and clearly you did not think to ask either."

Shaking her head in mild exasperation, Modan reached into the hollow once more and plucked out another berry, letting it rest on Sally's back.

"*This* is a crimson dewdrop," she explained, gently rolling it against the girl's soft, creamy skin to familiarize her with its texture. "They are quite sweet, but not what you were sent for."

SMACK! SMACK! SMACK! SMACK! SMCK!

Without warning, Modan delivered five full-force swats right against the relaxed mage's sit-spots, just as hard and fast as she could, sending the little berry flying off into the water as she began thrashing about.

"I'm sorry Mistress, I'm *sorry*! I wasn't thinking, I'm sorr-rryyyy!" wailed Sally, flailing her arms and legs wildly as she was taken by surprise.

"That often seems to be the case, little human," observed Modan, placing a firm hand on the girl's lower back as she waited for her to stop thrashing.

When her student had settled down again, she continued.

"This one is a morning star. Beloved of birds and bats, but poisonous to humans."

Sally stiffened as the naiad placed the berry in question along the base of her spine, noting the feel of its smaller, lighter, bumpier weight.

Oh horsefeathers! How could I have been so foolish? she berated herself silently.

SMACK! SMACK! SMACK! SMACK! SMACK!

She didn't have much time to dwell on her mistake however, for a moment later five more smacks exploded across her sit-spots, sending the scary berry flying and wringing out a fresh chorus of wails from her in the process.

"Ah! Oh! Ack!"

After she'd finished recovering from those swats, Sally heard Modan squish something between her fingers, and then felt cool, soothing juices dribbling down onto her sizzling cheeks. Sighing with relief at the wonderful sensation, she once more melted across the log as her mistress's strong fingers began to knead the juicy pulp gently into her sit-spots, up and down her cheeks, and along the inside of her crack. Her face flushed a hot shade of crimson as she felt the naiad's fingers spread her cheeks apart to work the juice in even further between them, and even around her puckered rosebud, but she didn't ask her to stop and instead buried her face in her hands while arching her back, purring softly with every caress.

Modan's fingers were relentless. Groping and squeezing everywhere they went, like a baker kneading dough, and the sensation was absolutely *breathtaking*.

"Oh Mistress… T-thank you!" she moaned.

Modan just smiled and kept on lovingly rubbing, working in more and more of the cold juices and taking in the adorable reactions of the girl across her lap. As she finished however, Sally started to grow aware of an unfamiliar tingling sensation that began to gradually supplant the cooling relief that she'd been feeling just a moment earlier.

"Those were six Kura's delights," Modan informed her, her voice carrying a cruel amusement with it. "Their burning oil fends off rot and fungi, but is harmless to the bats that eat them and spread their seeds."

Modan patted each cheek once, affectionately.

"I…"

Sally swallowed hard, feeling a thin sheen of sweat starting to form on her nervously furrowed brow.

"Um… I see."

There was a burn that followed in the aftermath of her

mistress's caress, one that had nothing to do with her earlier spanking. Sally's bottom and thighs suddenly felt *much* more sensitive, as if the air itself was enough to sting them, and she all too quickly found herself painfully aware of every single micro-current in the steam wafting across her bare skin.

Oh dear, I have a very bad feeling about this…

"Oh, and here are three more crimson dewdrops," announced Modan pleasantly, drawing Sally mercilessly out of her worried reverie as she returned to cracking her palm against her pupil's unprotected backside.

SMACK! SMACK! SMACK! SMACK! SMACK!

Again, without any warning whatsoever, she delivered fifteen hard, fast, and above all else merciless, spanks all over Sally's throbbing tush, setting the seemingly innocuous berry juices off like lantern oil from a spark!

"Aieee!"

Throwing her head back, Sally let out a long, high-pitched cry of agony, arching her spine and pushing her legs out as straight as they would go. If she hadn't known better, in those first few moments after Modan had started spanking her she would have *sworn* that she'd actually lit her bottom on fire with a spell! The burning sensation produced by those spanks landing on her berry juice soaked cheeks was absolutely, shockingly *exquisite* in its ferocity, and for nearly half a minute straight all she could do was squeal in shock and pain.

And then came the tears.

Ignoring her cries, Modan continued to merrily tick off the remaining berries she'd been presented with, delivering five vicious swats for each incorrect one she found.

"Let's see now… Five more morning stars, four dragonsbane eggs, and… oh my… *three* of my precious white rabbitberries!"

SMACK! SMACK! SMACK! SMACK! SMACK!

What ensued was pain far beyond any Sally had ever endured at the monastery, or even in the last day. The berry juice, already rubbed and spanked deep into her skin, was like a constant oil burn, and the seventy-five smacks that landed on top of her already ruby red bottom were thrice as painful as they should have been.

Gods below, she'd had no idea that that was even impossible!

Clinging to the root beneath her for dear life, Sally sobbed hysterically as Modan dished out a truly legendary spanking that pushed her well beyond what she thought she was capable of enduring. The pain was beyond words, and she soon found herself lost in a foggy sea of torment and fire for what felt like forever. It was the most intense punishment she'd ever experienced in her two and twenty years of life, and it was something that she would treasure always.

Once she had a chance to recover, that was.

—

Modan hoped that she would never have to spank the young mage like that ever again. Lots of *other* ways yes, but not like that. She let the girl cry for a time after she'd finished meting out her discipline, more than a little satisfied at having broken her down so completely, past words or struggles, submerging her fully into a deep lake of pain, submission, and acceptance.

With her punishment now over, she began massaging Sally's back softly and lovingly. And like dew embracing a leaf, she brought the mist around them inward and accumulated it around the poor girl's battered buttocks, moistening them and letting the irritating oil be washed away slowly, drop by drop.

Gradually, Sally's cheeks were revealed to now be a strikingly dark shade of crimson as the last of the berry pulp was carried away, not that far away from purple truth be told, and looked to be swollen to almost twice their usual size.

It wasn't a bad look at all, really. Probably better than the aftermath of any of the errant novice cultist punishments she'd witnessed, at least as far as she could remember.

"There, there," soothed Modan as she finally, *finally* crushed the seven great honeyberries that Sally had managed to collect for her and repeated the treatment from before, rubbing this much cooler, much softer juice into her ruined flesh.

It couldn't possibly relieve all of the pain she was feeling just then, that would require a prolonged soak in the waters of her bog to fully take effect, but it immediately took the edge off of it. She wanted Sally up and active again, to give her another chance to prove herself before nightfall.

—

Slowly, Sally began to emerge from her haze of agony and back into the land of the living. She was still sore and drained, feeling far more spent than she had after any prolonged training session she'd endured back at the monastery, but she at least no longer felt like her bottom was being held above a bonfire.

"You're a good girl."

Modan tickled her still hypersensitive cheeks and crack, and even the backs of her thighs for good measure, a low chuckle rumbling deep within her as she watched her spent student start squirming and giggling back into an approximation of her usual exuberance.

"A very thoughtless one sometimes, but good."

"T-thank you, Mistress," Sally managed to respond in a

breathy gasp as she wriggled in spite of herself, buoyed up by her mistress's kind words and wandering fingers. "I-I'm sorry I picked your special berries. Thank you for teaching me about them, though."

Modan responded by keeping up her kneading, ticking, and massaging. And after a while, she allowed one of her fingertips to venture downward and just *barely* tease the base of the girl's vulva. In turn, Sally's limbs jolted out in all directions, as if she'd just been struck by a bolt of lightning, and she let out a squeal that more than rivaled her ones from earlier.

"Ah! M-Mistress…" she moaned, gnawing on her lower lip as her eyes rolled up in pleasure and she once more went jelly-like across the naiad's spread thighs.

Modan ignored her reactions completely however, and continued to just rub and massage her bottom, thighs, and lower back. Pleased by the response she was getting, but not quite willing yet to let her desperate acolyte have the release she so clearly craved.

"Why don't you spend the rest of the daylight getting to know the plants and animals better?" she suggested gently, but firmly. "I think I've helped you learn enough to teach yourself some more on your own."

She patted her bottom a few times then, signaling that it was time to get up.

Sally let out a little whimper at the non-verbal order to rise, but nevertheless did as she was told and slowly slid off of the root and back into the warm water. The minerals and heat felt wonderful on her aching tush as it sank beneath the surface, although they did frustratingly little for her other ache.

Humph!

She was in no mood to earn any more discipline however,

and so with a nod of her head and a meek, "Yes Mistress", she sloshed off in the direction of the clusters of berries she'd pilfered earlier.

The first priority on her list of things to do was to get to know each and every one of those bushes and vines *very* well so that she never would have to experience their ill effects ever again!

Chapter 7

Dinner and Dessert

Sally Vinebrook did her very best to keep her sore and tender bottom submerged well beneath the surface of the warm, soothing, Power-saturated water as much as possible as she made her way around the bog. Over the course of the next several hours, she wandered happily from plant to plant and tree to tree, spending at least a few minutes (and often much longer) kneeling down beside each of them and getting to know them better, teasing out their particular quirks and characteristics while trying to memorize the feel of their auras within the tapestry of the Power. It was slow and careful work, requiring meticulous attention to detail, and Sally absolutely *adored* it.

Her only regret was that she'd completely forgotten to bring her sketchbook and charcoal pencils along with her to Modan's bog, having left them behind in her saddlebags with Bella.

Oh well, they probably would have just gotten all soggy anyway, she told herself with a carefree shrug, popping a couple of honeyberries into her mouth before sloshing off in search of some of those dragonsbane eggs her mistress had mentioned. *I'll just have to commit as much of this as I can to memory and then write it all down later when I get the chance.*

By the time dusk had begun to settle on the deceptively peaceful and sleepy swamp, Sally's bottom had been restored more or less back to its pale and un-punished state. Her cheeks were once again silky smooth to the touch and free of welts and bruises, and now only sported a faint touch of pink on their undercurves. They were still tender, but now she only felt as if she'd received a mild spanking earlier that afternoon, instead of the mother of all bottom burners she'd actually experienced.

Who would have ever suspected that such a small berry could pack such a powerful burn? Kura's delight indeed, humph!

As an educated Cindertouched, Sally knew much about Kura, the lord of stone and fire, and father of dragons. It was he who had Touched her before she was born and woven her into his weave of the Power. But she had never heard of this particular berry that bore his namesake, and she couldn't help but feel that he was being unfairly maligned by the association. Still, based on the sensations the berries had caused, she had to admit it was *somewhat* appropriate.

Brimming with barely controlled enthusiasm over all the new and wondrous things that she'd been able to see and interact with since she'd been turned loose to study, Sally returned to Modan's side just as the patchwork sky seen through the canopy above was starting to turn crimson and declared with a little twirl and a splash, "I'm back, Mistress!"

"You never left," came Modan's smooth reply a moment later as she rose just as smoothly from where she'd been lounging in the murky depths some five feet ahead of her pupil, looking somehow even more fresh and elegant than she had earlier that morning.

Sally smirked playfully at the naiad's literalness and rolled her eyes.

"It's just an expression, you know. Of course I didn't *actually* leave."

She felt an exhilarating little twinge of butterflies in her stomach as the words left her mouth, and she surreptitiously crossed her fingers behind her back in the hope that the naiad wouldn't interpret her teasing as her being impolite. The mere thought of the spanking she'd received earlier for being rude about mutton during their midday meal still made her knees wobble. Though thankfully, that wasn't particularly noticeable with the waterline hiding most of her body below the waist.

"Well now, someone sure seems *awfully* confident in themselves," observed Modan with a wry chuckle as she glided toward the young mage, closing to within arm's reach without so much as a whisper of turbulence on the water to mark her passing. "Why don't you tell me what you've learned since our last conversation?"

She paused for a heartbeat, and then smiled.

"Or better yet, show me."

Sally's stomach fluttered even harder as Modan drew close to her, her worry warring with her excitement over what might happen next should she keep sassing the naiad. She was also eager to impress however, and beaming brightly, she pointed over to a pair of bushes a few feet away whose branches were brimming heavily with fat, round, red berries.

"*Those* are Kura's delight bushes! They were the first ones I tracked down," she proclaimed with a half-pout half-scowl. "They're actually very nice plants to talk to, despite how mean their berries can be."

Modan laughed pleasantly.

"The berries aren't mean, silly girl. They just don't like to be eaten by bugs. And I'm not surprised you befriended them. They did seem to be your favorite."

Sally squirmed a little in the shallows as memories of just how appropriately named those seemingly innocent little berries were rushed through her mind.

"I like honeyberries better," she mumbled with a pout.

"You could have fooled me," replied Modan with a predatory grin, sliding in beside her and laying a firm hand on her shoulder. "I heard you gasping and sighing while I rubbed those fat, red berries all over your fat, red tush. Hmmm… I'll bet you'd just *love* some more right now, wouldn't you?"

"Eep!"

In response to her taunting question, Sally's face began to glow about as red and as hot as the berries on the bushes she was staring fixedly at, and a small squeak escaped her lips. Part of her wanted to lie to the naiad, to vehemently claim that she totally hated the experience, but deep down she knew that she couldn't (and *really* shouldn't), so she forced herself to admit, "T-they were, um… rather pleasant, at first, I suppose… Nice and, um…"

She felt a fresh pulse of nervous delight throb along the also pouting lips between her squirming thighs.

"Warm."

And your hands rubbing me all over back there sure didn't hurt either!

Modan just chuckled.

"Well then, I'll be sure to give you some more sometime soon. Perhaps tomorrow? Or perhaps the next day?"

Shifting around to stand behind her, she let her other hand that wasn't busy massaging the mage's tense shoulder dip down beneath the water to gently fondle the area where those berries would be applied, retaining an innocent grin all the while.

Oh horsefeathers and dragon spit! wailed Sally internally as she felt her heart leap and her thighs press themselves together under the murk. *I was just trying to be honest! What did I just talk myself into?*

"What else have you learned?" asked Modan, bringing her lips right beside the quivering girl's right ear to murmur the question while keeping the palm of her hand resting meaningfully against her bum.

Looking for any excuse to not dwell on the Kura's delight bush and its confusingly arousing berries, Sally cast her eyes around for another plant to talk about, and a moment later pointed to one with small clumps of bumpy little berries clustered all over it.

"Those are morning stars!" she announced hurriedly. "They're nice too. It's just a shame that I can't eat their berries, though. I'm sure they'd be tasty, and that people would love to plant them in their gardens"

"I already told you about those," purred the naiad, her breath tickling Sally's ear as her fingertips flexed warningly against her left cheek. "Show me something I haven't told you. Something you've used what I've taught you to uncover on your own."

She was clearly testing her pupil now, but there was no judgment in her voice. Just guidance.

Sally grimaced as it began to dawn on her that she'd spent most of the time allotted to her for studying making idle chit-chat with plants, and she racked her mind for an idea.

"Um…"

She frowned in concentration, idly digging her toes into the silt beneath her feet.

"Oh!"

Smiling eagerly, her earlier exuberance restored, she pointed to one of the fat dragonflies circling lazily over the steamy water.

"I noticed something peculiar about the flying insects around here."

She paused for a moment to look down at the gently glowing worm that had now petrified into a proper ring around her third finger, gathering her thoughts and growing somewhat pensive as she attempted to organize her observations into a coherent idea.

"They aren't as imbued with the Power as the things that live *inside* the water, or at least spend a lot of their time nearby it are. I think it's because they only stay in it until they hatch, and then they fly away."

"That is correct," confirmed the naiad with an approving nibble against her ear. "They spend less time with me here, and more time high in the trees or flying around the bog. Because of this, there is less of me in them and as a result they don't *obey me* quite as readily."

Modan gripped Sally's bottom a little tighter under the water to emphasize her point then.

"Now, why don't you demonstrate your new understanding for me? Bring us some dinner."

"Dinner?" squeaked Sally, wriggling in her mistress's grip as the corners of her mouth quirked up in a shy smile. "Um… r-right! I can do that."

Truth be told, she wasn't *actually* so sure about that. She could definitely gather as many honeyberries as either of them could ever possibly want to eat (she'd been snacking on them off and on all afternoon), but berries alone seemed like a poor meal and a less than ideal way to show off just how much she'd been learning.

"Hmmm…"

She looked down at the water thoughtfully for several long moments, and then an idea struck her. Closing her eyes and centering her mind within the Power, she pushed out her perception to the creatures and plants all around her, looking for… crabs.

She quickly found a small cluster of them not too far off from where they stood, and focusing in on the small group of crustaceans milling about on top of one another beneath the surface, she ever so gently coaxed out a telepathic thought toward them, adding as much Power behind it as she dared.

Ahem. Excuse me, uh… crabs… Silt to part beneath spurs of bone, ripples hot from Deep Mother's throne, I call you with rot, with stone, with fear, your path through the bounties of death is clear.

She whispered the words of Power to send the message away through the cascading weave of connections that riddled the bog, and then paused for a moment. Nervously.

So, um, would you all come here for a moment please?

It took a little bit longer than she'd hoped it would, but Sally felt a huge sigh of relief escape her as at last some soft-shelled crustaceans came scuttling up to crawl and probe around their feet on the silty bottom of the sandbar.

"You were paying attention in the charax cave, I see," observed Modan with a broad smile. "You listened to what he was telling them, and you did the same. Very good."

Quick as a flash and with her usual fluid grace, she disappeared beneath the water for a brief moment, and then came back up holding a crab in each hand.

"Let me guess. You went back to the entrance and listened again?"

"That's right, Mistress," confirmed Sally, nodding her head and looking just a bit bashful.

It seemed like a waste of the temporary gift she'd been given not to make the most of it.

She cast her eyes back toward the tree that marked the entrance to the old charax's root-cavern, and a soft smile played across her delicate features.

"At first I thought he was rather scary, but he's actually alright. Even if he is a little bit, um…"

She gestured vaguely, seeming to be reaching for a polite way of phrasing her thoughts.

"*Focused* on eating."

The old charax hadn't made the best conversation partner, but he'd at least been fascinating to watch.

Modan shook her head a little at that, smiling in bemusement.

"No charax has ever harmed a human, except perhaps by pinching one's toes. Of course, it's very rare for a human to meet a truly old one."

With that, she gave the mage's bottom one final squeeze and then glided over to a small island of smooth stone half-buried in mud and sticks in a small clearing between the trees. Stepping out of the thigh-high water, she crossed to the center of it and knelt down on the flat surface, patting a spot beside her.

"Come. Let's eat here."

Beaming to herself at the thought of having seen such a rare sight up close not once, but *twice*, Sally followed after the naiad and joined her on the little island. She eyed the soft, muddy ground appraisingly, prodding a few twigs and loose rocks out of the way with her toe, and then carefully eased herself down. Her bottom was still a little tender, after all, and sitting down made her wince, but it was just a minor discomfort (one that made her blush if she thought about it for too long) rather than an actual pain. Plus the cool mud being smooshed against her sensitive backside made for a nice change of pace from the bubbly warmth of the lake.

"Ahhh, that's lovely."

As she cooked her crab the same way as earlier in the day, pacing herself this time instead of flash-frying it all at once, Sally happened to notice the oddly rectangular shape of the little stone island that Modan had chosen for them to sit on.

"Hmmm…" she murmured to herself, leaning forward and squinting her eyes for a closer inspection.

Sure enough, the mud-filled cracks in the places where the water had worn away most of the siltation appeared to be geometric, if badly weathered. One of the stones even had a faint imprint on it, as if from an ancient carving, though it was badly worn and most of it was covered in a thick layer of mud now.

One by one, the pieces slowly began to fall into place inside Sally's mind as she brushed away some of the grime, and a moment later she felt her eyes grow wide as saucers as her memory flashed back to the other oddly geometric and uniformly spaced stones that she'd seen earlier while underwater.

"A temple!" she exclaimed, spitting out bits of tasty crab meat (she'd managed to not overcook hers this time) and jumping to her feet, dancing from foot to foot excitedly. "We're standing on a temple! On top of *your* temple, Mistress!"

Then, realizing that she'd just tossed aside all of her table manners in her moment of discovery, she quickly plopped back down onto her backside and added in a far more restrained voice, "Um… right?"

"We've been swimming through it ever since I returned to you," answered Modan with a nod as she nonchalantly sucked down some of her own crab. "This was once one of the altars."

Eying the stones beneath them with a newfound awe, Sally traced her fingertips carefully along their worn surface. Then, with a squeak, she scrambled up to her knees and began fumbling around in the mud in search of bits of spat out crab meat while she babbled in a rush.

"Oh horsefeathers, I am *so* sorry, Mistress! I didn't mean to be rude and just sit on your altar like it was a chair. Please forgive me!"

Sally had visited the chapels in her home town and at the Celestine Monastery innumerable times, of course, and stopped at a dozen travelers' shrines since beginning her journeyman period, but she'd only ever been inside a *temple* once before. That one visit, along with her reading, was enough for her to know that you were *supposed* to be respectful and on your best behavior inside of them, *not* lounge about like they were the common room of some inn!

"I'm sitting on it," was Modan's unconcerned reply as she continued sucking away at her crab with cool amusement. "And I highly doubt that there's any structure that would mind having *your* bottom pressed against it."

She giggled a little mischievously at that before continuing.

"Besides, this was my mother's altar, not mine. So, apologize to her if you think you need to."

Sally still felt more than a little apprehensive about using the once sacred and well-maintained offering platform as a makeshift table, but since Modan seemed to be smiling and giggling, she decided that it was probably alright for her to relax as well. And so, with a long exhalation, she flopped back down onto the cool mud once again, and winced as she was sharply reminded that her bottom was still somewhat sore. She then picked up her crab, and after brushing off a few flecks of mud stuck to its side, returned to nibbling on it as she inspected her surroundings more closely.

The altar was clearly old, *very* old, but then again its appearance could also have just been due to it having been partially submerged underwater for so long now. Mother

Nature certainly had a talent for swallowing up the handi-work of mortals if left to her own devices, after all. Intrigued, Sally mulled the whole situation over as she chewed and swallowed mechanically, no longer noticing the succulent flavor of the roasted crab in her hands as she took slow, careful bites.

Several minutes later, she wiped her mouth with the back of her hand and asked, "Why is your mother's temple gone? Where is she? Did she move?"

Once more tapping a thoughtful forefinger against the side of her cheek, Sally stared off into space as she tried to wrap her mind around such a concept.

"*Can* a water nymph just pack up and move somewhere else?"

Modan laughed again at her litany of questions, much louder this time.

"My mother never went anywhere. She's still in the great, watery cavern below us."

She then adopted a more sober expression as she went on.

"And no, I cannot move from here. Nor would I ever wish to any more than a human would tire of breathing air or drinking water."

"I see…" murmured Sally, idly nibbling on her thumbnail now as she added this new bit of information to her mental notes.

"And as to your other question…"

Modan gave her an unconcerned shrug.

"I don't know why the people stopped coming. It was a very long time ago, and I don't remember that very well."

She had taken on the most serious expression Sally had seen on her yet as she spoke, aside for her most punitive moments of strictness perhaps. Sally's own crab lay completely forgotten now as her imagination ran wild trying to picture what it must have been like back when this bog had been a thriving place of worship. In her mind's eye she could see neat rows of white pillars supporting sharp-angled stone ceilings with intricate carvings adorning every available surface, and acolytes of all ages running to and fro among well-kept gardens attending to the business of their daily worship. Surely it must have been a marvel to behold!

So what had changed all that?

"Surely you must remember *something* though, Mistress," she pressed gently.

"Not really," Modan explained patiently, staring off into the mist as if gazing back upon a long forgotten age. "As I said, I can recall very little. I remember that the sacrifices became less and less frequent over time. Fewer children came to join the cult, and soon it was only a few old men and women who tended to the flowers and offered prayer and sacrifice for the occasional visitor. Parts of the temple were already sinking into the mud by the time the last of the old cultists had finally left, and the rest fell into ruin soon after."

Finishing her story, she sucked the last of her crab legs dry and with a casual flick of her wrist sent the empty shell sailing into the water where several little fish immediately began to swarm around it.

"And that's all there is for me to tell."

Although it had been delivered with her usual casual sternness, Modan's story had touched Sally. Staring at her mistress with watery eyes, she said in as sober a voice as she could muster, "I'm so sorry to hear that, Mistress. That must have been very lonely for you."

Then, not sure what else to do, but knowing what always made *her* feel better when she was feeling down, she scooted in closer and wrapped the damp naiad in a tight hug.

"It wasn't lonely." replied Modan matter-of-factly, a bit bemused by the young mage's sudden embrace, but doing nothing to stop her. "I have the charaxes and knuckers and trees for company. Not to mention the birds and the bats, as well. Sometimes I simply lie in the hot spring and listen to my mother's songs for years on end."

She smiled a little comfortingly, and wrapped one strong arm around the girl's naked shoulders, returning her embrace.

"Of course, *you* need other humans, or human-like things, to help you survive. You'd be miserable if you were away from others like yourself for that long. I'm different, though."

She gave her armful of tender mage flesh a reassuring squeeze then.

"There were no people here for many centuries before the temple, and there haven't been for many since. I liked them, while they were here, but I never *needed* them."

Sally snuggled happily in against her mistress's slick warmth, and smiled into her shoulder.

Despite our physical similarities, she really is quite different from me, isn't she?

Once again, she found herself drawn to just how fascinating and unique Modan really was.

At least I didn't do anything to inadvertently offend her this time!

She let herself be held in in the naiad's embrace without saying anything for as long as she dared to, just enjoying the feel of her skin against hers and the weight of her strong arm around her shoulders.

Eventually though, she felt like she needed to say *something*, so she murmured, "I think I understand now, Mistress. Thank you for explaining."

"Mmhmm. Now finish your crab. I'll be cross if I killed it

for nothing, you know."

Modan fixed Sally with a stern glare, but then just as quickly eased back into a teasing smile and a fit of giggles when she saw the apprehension her words produced in the jumpy little mage.

With her stomach flip-flopping with butterflies born from the stern look in her mistress's dark eyes, and then exacerbated by her teasing smile, Sally untangled herself from around Modan and scooted back over to where her crab lay on the mud-covered stone. Scooping it up, she brushed it off with her fingertips once again and blew a few stubborn clumps of dirt off of it, and then resumed eating it with a newfound dedication that had nothing to do with hunger. If her mistress told her to finish her meal, then she was going to finish her meal.

Especially if there was a punishment on the line if she didn't!

"So," she asked between bites, nodding her chin in the direction of the boiling hot spring on the central island of the lake clearing. "How come your mother hasn't come up to say hello yet? Does she not like visitors?"

Modan simply looked back at her, bemused.

"Come up here?"

"Right!" replied Sally with an eager bob of her head. "I've never met the mother of a water nymph before, and it *would* be rather rude of me to have spent as much time as I have here without at least greeting her properly..."

Munch. Munch.

Modan continued staring at the girl with something akin to disbelief as she dutifully chewed her crab meat.

"My mother only shows herself to mortals on very, *very* important occasions."

Modan paused to think for a moment then.

"Come to think of it, I don't actually know when the last time was. Maybe when the sun refused to shine? No, it was later than that…"

She tilted her head to the side and let out a low hum of concentration.

"Or was it when the demons behind the eclipse invaded? Perhaps… After all, she *was* among those who rose up to repel them…"

Modan paused again, and then continued more confidently this time.

"At any rate, she sung to me not too long ago about a city called Talinasia where a prophet of hers dwells. Perhaps she's been there recently?"

"Oh… oh my…" breathed Sally in awed wonder.

Of course she knew of the great temple of Artthun in Talinasia. Who didn't?

"I um… I hadn't realized your mother was so, um… so…"

*I hadn't realized your mother was literally **the** river goddess!* she thought to herself in utter astonishment, growing uncomfortably aware of just how naked and fragile she was just then. *Horsefeathers and dragon spit, Sally! What kind of a fool just casually asks for an audience with the honest to goodness river goddess of all people?*

Swallowing hard, she tried desperately to work some saliva back into her suddenly very, very dry mouth.

"I… um y-yes, I know all about the temple in T-Talinasia… It's a, uh…"

She cleared her throat and swallowed once more.

"A w-well-known landmark of modern c-civilization after all… Um… S-sorry Mistress, I didn't mean to, um… to overstep my boundaries…"

Modan laughed again, shaking her head and sending her long, tangly, wet tresses all about.

"I'm starting to think you don't actually *have* any boundaries to overstep, little human."

Still giggling, she added in mock seriousness.

"Do you need another spanking already?"

Sally's cheeks flushed a hot scarlet at the question and she stared fixedly down at her fidgeting hands on her lap.

"Um... I um..."

It *should* have been a simple question to answer. All she had to say was "No, no, that's fine!", but... Instead she forced herself to look up to meet the enchanting pull of her mistress's liquid gaze.

"M-maybe..."

"Maybe?"

Modan grinned and leaned forward, making her large silhouette almost predatory.

"Well *I* think you do."

She was still grinning as she said it, her eyes sparkling with laughter. Bringing one knee forward, she began to crawl toward her naughty student, a hungry smile pulled tight across her soft, blue lips.

"So tell me, my wise, young acolyte, how do you think I should spank you for this particular offense? Hmmm?"

"Eep!"

The squeak escaped from Sally's lips before she could stop it, her heart nearly jumping out of her mouth right along with it as she watched her mistress begin to bear down on her.

"M-M-M-M-Mistress, I-I..." she spluttered, her face turning an even darker shade of red as she tried to squeeze the words out from between her trembling lips.

"I asked you a question, *girl*," came Modan's low reply as she kneed her way across the mud and stones until she was right in front of Sally, her large, round breasts hanging freely just below the girl's blushing, wide-eyed face. "You *know* I don't like it when you refuse to answer me."

She was still grinning, with a hungry, narrow-eyed gaze that had the poor mage rooted to the spot.

"Well?"

Leaning in even further, she cupped a warm, damp hand against the back of Sally's warm, damp hair, while her other began to play lazily up and down along her shoulder and back.

"Answer me."

"Y-Yes Mistress! Sorry Mistress!" squeaked Sally, the words bubbling out of her in a rush as her stomach churned in near constant flip-flops.

Modan was just so close! She could actually *feel* the heat radiating off of the naiad's powerful body as her fingertips tickled her between her shoulder blades! She knew she was supposed to give her an answer, but she just couldn't focus long enough to figure out what she should say.

Then, in a moment of perfect clarity, a deliciously naughty idea came to her.

Clearing her throat with a nervous cough, she scooted back a couple of paces from her mistress and rose up onto wobbly knees as she turned her back on her. Then, with one last shaky exhalation, she carefully bent her torso forward until her naked breasts were pressed firmly into the cool mud beneath her, with her nipples scraping lightly against the smooth stone underneath. She then slowly and tentatively pushed her hips up and back, higher and higher, arching her back and parting her knees just enough so that her bare bottom and everything in between was on full display for Modan, presenting herself to her mistress as if she were a sacrifice for her altar.

"P-Please Mistress," she stuttered out while hiding her burning face behind her trembling forearms. "P-Punish me as… as you see fit!"

"Oh, I will."

—

Modan chuckled again, taking a few moments to silently admire the big, still pink and faintly marked cheeks being offered up on the altar like the sacrifices of old (although none of them were ever so jiggly). Reveling in how the young human dutifully held them in place for her appraisal, despite her nervous shivering.

Truly, a worthy offering.

Closing in another pace, she began to glide her fingernails up and down across the chubby curves, enjoying the feel of their plump springiness and the parade of gooseflesh that trailed after wherever she touched. She then gently gripped a tender cheek in each hand and spread them apart, fully exposing all of the girl's charms to the light caress of the warm mist. With a low chuckle, she spent a few moments tickling the inner slopes of her cleft, her fingers teasingly stopping just millimeters away from her little bottom hole and the base of her vulva, before slowly easing her buns back together, rubbing each cheek one final time, and then delivering the first hearty swat.

SMACK!

"Ah!"

—

Lost as she was in her mistress's gentle caresses and trying not to giggle as her sensitive cheeks were played with, the first spank came as a total surprise to Sally.

Although it probably shouldn't have.

Still though, she managed to keep her hips raised and in place like they were supposed to be. She *was* a good girl after all.

With a throaty moan, she hissed in a breath of warm air through clenched teeth, savoring the stinging heat in right cheek where Modan's palm had just struck.

"T-Thank you, Mistress…"

"Hold still," ordered Modan imperiously, "You have many more to come."

She gently fondled and squeezed the spot she'd just spanked, and then a moment later spanked it again!

SMACK!

"Ah! Y-yes Mistress!" gasped Sally, squirming on her knees in the mud and moaning, but otherwise maintaining her position as ordered.

More fondling quickly followed, and then a moment later there came another spank, this time on the other cheek.

SMACK!

Then came more fondling, and then it was back to the other cheek for another meaty swat.

SMACK!

After that, Modan began to fondle the trembling girl's arched sit-spots, using both of her hands to squeeze and rub them at her leisure. At this, Sally finally lost it, and a fit of giggles bubbled up from behind her folded arms.

"What's so funny?" demanded Modan.

SMACK-SMACK! SMACK-SMACK!

She swatted the giggling mage four more times in quick

succession, much harder than she had before, twice on each cheek. However, her voice was still mirthful, not angry.

Sally in turn yelped and wriggled at these harder swats, her hips swaying hypnotically from side to side with each one as she struggled (and mostly succeeded) to maintain her position.

"Sorry Mistress!" she squeaked. "You were ticking me. I wasn't laughing at you, I promise!"

Modan watched the swinging buns before her like a cat tracking the movements of a piece of string. Pouncing, she grabbed the girl's waist firmly with one hand and delivered ten more swats, hard like the last four, before stopping and lightly squeezing the fatty undercurve of her right cheek.

"You're very ticklish, aren't you?" she asked, tracing up and down her acolyte's crack with a pair of wiggling fingerstips. "Maybe I need to beat that out of you?"

SMACK!

Again she slapped a jiggly sit-spot, and then went back to tickling her crack.

"Oh pleeeease, Mistress," moaned Sally between breathy gasps, the naiad's tickling, fondling, and spanking reducing her to a panting, wriggling mess as she tried desperately to maintain her position for her.

"Perhaps I'll hang you from the trees with your arms and legs splayed out, and make the vines tickle you with their softest leaves."

Modan swatted again.

SMACK!

"And switch your big, round bottom until you stop laughing."

She swatted three more times, hard.

SMACK! SMACK! SMACK!

And then went right back to fondling.

"Would that cure you, naughty girl?"

"I- Hah! I… d-d-don't- Hah- Owie! Th- Oh! think that w-will ch- Oooh! change anything!" gasped Sally between laughs and yelps, trying, and failing miserably, to keep her squirming and giggling under control.

And I most definitely don't want those stupid vines getting hold of me again. They've been making fun of me all after-noon. Humph!

"I don't think so either, really." admitted Modan.

She was slapping at an even cadence now, stinging and burning the moaning mage's wobbly bottom a little bit hotter with each swat, while still occasionally stopping for a brief rub.

"But we will try anyway."

She started slapping faster then, cinching her arm once again around Sally's waist to hold her in place as she delivered one swat to each squirming sit-spot, and then one directly to the semi-parted center of the girl's behind.

SMACK-SMACK! SMACK! SMACK-SMACK! SMACK!

"Perhaps an extra-strong dose of Kura's delights will help you maintain your composure better, hmmm? You *did* say you wanted to feel them again, you know. Now *that* would be rather effective, I'm sure."

She laughed again, and then raised her arm even higher to give more dramatic, loud swats.

SMACK-SMACK! SMACK! SMACK-SMACK! SMACK!

"Not to mention entertaining."

"Oh *please*, Mistress," moaned Sally, not even sure what exactly she was pleading for anymore as she drummed her toes into the mud and bucked her hips in the water nymph's inescapable iron grip.

Her bottom was already pleasantly hot, and was growing

steadily hotter with each sharp spank, while her mind swam through a haze of panic, embarrassment, delight, and excitement.

"Please what?" prompted Modan as she continued swatting.

But Sally just chewed on her lower lip and let out another long moan, stubbornly refusing to answer the question.

"Answer me!"

SMACK-SMACK! SMACK-SMACK! SMACK-SMACK!

Modan started spanking for real then, hard and fast, just like she had earlier in the day. And when her errant student started to struggle in earnest, she simply dug her elbow into her back, mashing her face and breasts even deeper into the earthy ground as her right hand became a blur, going straight for sit-spots and upper thighs.

"*Aieee!*" squealed Sally, all thoughts of trying to ride out her embarrassing thoughts and take her punishment stoically flying out the window as she began to let loose with high-pitched cries of pain. "M-Mistress, please! I'm going to… I'm going to!"

Instead of finishing her sentence, she thrust her hips up even higher, squeezing and rubbing her thighs together with increased urgency as an entirely different inferno of need built up between them.

In response, Modan sat down heavily next to the moaning mage, and pulled her gracelessly over her muddy lap. Heedless of her squiggles and squeals, she started into an over the knee spanking no less hard than the one from the day before, but considerably slower and with a great deal more grasping and groping between swats.

SMACK…! SMACK…! SMACK…!

Once again Sally's high-pitched penitent wails began to

echo into the mist. This new position over her mistress's lap did little to mitigate her rapidly building arousal, and if anything made it much, much worse since she now had a firm thigh to grind herself against. With each swat and grope, the mental image of her hanging suspended while vines tickled and lashed her naked body grew more and more vivid in her mind's eye, leaving her more breathless and excited by the second! She was lost in a swirling vortex of conflicting emotions, and had no idea how to articulate her thoughts in a way that would satisfy Modan. And in the end she simply cried out with a blush so hot that she feared her hair might catch aflame as she moaned.

"Mistress please! Please punish me! Do with me as you will, I promise to obey!"

And Modan did just that, swatting her hard, and hot, and long.

—

When Modan finally stopped spanking, Sally's bottom was almost as red as it had been that morning, and she lay gasping and dewy-eyed across her lap.

"Hmmm… I think I would like some dessert now," she declared suddenly, swatting Sally's rump extra-hard, directly across its center, one last time.

SMACK!

"Get up."

Breathing heavily and rubbing at her burning hindquarters with one hand and her watery eyes with the back of the other, Sally climbed up off of Modan's lap and knelt beside her.

"Dessert, Mistress?" she asked with a sniffle, taking special care to ensure that her sizzling cheeks didn't accidentally come into contact with her heels as she cast her eyes about for the nearest bunch of honeyberries.

Instead of answering however, Modan just stood up abruptly and grabbed Sally by the scruff of her neck, hauling her brusquely into the water.

"That root!" she growled, pointing to a thick root protruding from the base of a nearby tree, half-in and half-out of the twilight murk. "Grab onto it, and don't you *dare* let go."

Releasing the girl's neck, she gave her an especially vicious swat to get her moving.

SMACK!

"Yes Mi- *Eek!*" squeaked Sally, her words gobbled up in a high-pitched yelp as she scrambled through the water and tumbled forward at a sharp angle to grab hold of the sinewy branch.

Modan pounced on her half a heartbeat later, seizing her roughly by the shoulders and neck and smooshing her big, soft body against hers under and out of the water as she growled in her ear.

"Now pray to my mother. Pray like the cultists once did. And do *not* stop."

She then slid into the water behind the girl, her hands gliding down along either of her flanks as she sank beneath the surface.

Sally shuddered as bolts of electricity shot through her at her mistress's gruff words and caresses, but she dared not disobey. For a few heart-stopping moments she tried to remember the chants and key phrases of the old prayers she'd seen written in books, her mind swimming as worries over what might happen if she couldn't remember them sizzled through her, before finally starting to murmur shakily.

"Oh mighty Artthun, Mistress of the Rivers, and Mother of the Streams... This humble and, um... unworthy servant beseeches thee!"

As this was happening, Modan submerged herself completely.

Settling down onto her knees between the mage and the root, she pulled Sally's thighs apart, sliding her large hands between them and groping their creamy interiors just below the girl's groin.

"A-ah!" cried Sally, as her mistress's nimble fingers found purchase below the waterline.

Swallowing hard, she chewed on her lower lip for several moments, before finally managing to continue in an even more shaky voice.

"H-h-hallowed be thy divine name… th-this servant humbly c-calls upon thee t-to, to…"

Horsefeathers! How did it go again?

"Oh! To visit thy mercy upon th-the crops of the fields, and th-the wells of our lands…!"

As the mage began to pick up steam again, Modan moved her fingers up to dig into her burning sit-spots, and slid her face between her thighs; giving Sally a second kiss, much deeper than the last one, on her other set of lips. She pawed at her swollen little bud in its sheath with her lips, and dabbed at it with her rough, yet silky, tongue under the warm water. She then pulled her thighs even further apart, and began to move her mouth up and down, from clitoris to crevice, kissing, licking, and sucking strategically at both.

"H-h-horsefeathers!" moaned Sally in both pain from the rough handling of her sore sit-spots, and ecstasy as her mistress's mouth probed and caressed her aching vagina, all thoughts of anything other than sensation scoured from her mind as lightning bolts of pleasure radiated out from her swollen lower lips.

The sensation was overwhelming, reducing her knees to jelly and causing her to slump forward. Clinging to the root in front of her for dear life, she tried desperately to get her tongue to wrap itself around the next part of the prayer.

"D... d... drive b-back... the... t-t-the scouuuurge!"

Modan dug her fingernails in even more cruelly, utterly heedless of the pain in Sally's cheeks. As the mage squealed, she began tonguing her deeply, as if famished and starving for her womanhood. She nibbled on the sheath of her clit, and then lashed it ruthlessly with her tongue to punish it for emerging. She then let her fingers take over there and moved her lips back down, writhing her tongue as deep into the gasping girl as it could go while her other hand kept squeezing and clawing at her swollen cheeks.

Sally's vision flashed white, and cries of ecstasy came flying out of her like birds taking wing. Gasping and moaning, she writhed in her mistress's grasp, wriggling her hips and pushing them against her busy mouth, silently begging for more. She *tried* to continue the prayer, but the feel of Modan's tongue wriggling around inside of her while she expertly pinched and rolled her clitoris between her thumb and forefinger was too much for her to handle, and all that managed to bubble out of her was a throaty gurgle of, "M-M-M-Mistress!"

Nimble as a seal underwater, Modan flipped around underneath Sally and brought her face up behind her ruby rump. Still seizing and clawing at her cheeks, she roughly pulled them apart and, after lashing her pussy a bit more, began circling her tongue around her tiny, little bottom hole. She kept this up until the mage was trembling like a leaf in the wind, and then brought her lips to it and *very* slowly started to force her tongue inside, lashing and flicking it against her insides as she penetrated her rear.

Sally's eyes shot open at that, growing wide as saucers as a crimson flush climbed up her neck all the way to the roots of her muddy blonde hair.

"M-Mistress n-no, you can't!" she squealed, clenching her bottom reflexively (and uselessly) in Modan's iron grip.

She didn't actually mean it of course. Although it was an entirely new experience for her, being taken in her behind felt surprisingly good, but another person's tongue was the last thing she'd ever thought would be pushed inside of there! The thought of it was so exhilarating and embarrassing, that all she could do was heat up the water around her to boiling with her blush, temporarily losing control of her Cindertouched gifts and her grip on the Power as she panted and moaned in near-overwhelming pleasure.

In response to her futile resistance, Modan suddenly pulled her mouth back, and bit down on the reddest part of Sally's right sit-spot.

Hard.

Painfully hard.

Sally immediately caught the meaning: "I can do whatever I want. Now keep praying." and crying out in pain again, even as a fresh ripple of lightning charged up her spine, she threw back her head and began to shout out her exhortations.

"Drive back the scourge! And bring forth the spring!"

Satisfied, Modan went back to tonguing her rosebud deeply and fiercely, finding the back of the girl's g-spot and lashing it as if her tongue were one of her whipping vines.

Sally screamed again, though this time not in pain, as explosions of ecstasy were set off behind her clenched eyelids and her toes curled tightly around the muddy silt beneath her feet.

"M-m-may your b-blessing… May your blessing s-sh-shine on us all! F-f-for time everlasting! Th-this servant prays, a-amen!"

Modan didn't stop after Sally finished her prayer, instead going back to her pussy and letting a finger take over the other job in her bum, and then back again a while later. On and on she went, devouring the girl without mercy and drowning her in a tumultuous sea of orgasmic bliss.

—

When she had at last been fully sated, Modan simply floated behind Sally and held her, hugging her gently, but tightly, in a warm embrace, and resting her strong chin on her shoulder.

Sally's breath was coming in great ragged gasps by the time it was all over, her body wreathed in a fine sheen of sweat as if she were trying to imitate her mistress's own skin as she let herself be cradled in her strong arms. It took several very long minutes before she was able to regain control of her breathing and once again organize her thoughts into something coherent.

Smiling dreamily as they floated listlessly through the mist, she sighed.

"Mistress…"

"Yes, my dear?"

"That was…" Sally swallowed and wet her lips, groping for the right words, before sighing again and simply saying. "That was, *amazing.*"

Modan didn't reply, and instead just floated behind her, holding her until she fully recovered.

Then, finally she said, "It has been a very long time since that ritual was performed here. You did it well, though your words were strange to me."

She nibbled affectionately at Sally's earlobe as she spoke,

and then kissed her cheek.

"Tell me. Have you ever given pleasure before, sweet mage?"

Giggling at the nibble and smiling at her mistress's kiss, Sally felt her tongue trip over itself as she admitted shyly, "J-just a little bit with my fingers by myself a couple of times and with some of my fellow sisters back at the monastery…"

She swallowed and blushed again.

"I'm not sure if I can, um… measure up to your level, Mistress…"

"Then I will simply have to teach you, as I said I would," came Modan's matter-of-fact reply, as she reached up both hands and began to fondle Sally's breasts and tease their sensitive nipples. "You will show me what you know, and I will punish you if I deem it inadequate."

She pinched the girl's erect nipples then, smiling cruelly at the throaty gasp-moan doing so produced in her.

"Then I will show you how to do it better, and you will try again."

Modan nibbled the crook of Sally's neck, savoring the taste of her as her fingers continued to tweak and twist.

"And I will punish you again and again and *again* until I have been *fully* pleasured. How does that sound to you, my sweet, little human?"

Chewing on her lower lip, Modan's words filling her with that delicious sense of dread and anticipation that she seemed capable of producing in her whenever she felt like it, Sally nodded her head and let out another moan.

"Y-yes Mistress, I'll do my best! Please teach me!"

In response to her earnest plea, vines coiled down from the branches overhead, wrapping themselves around the two of them and hauling them up into the canopy. Hours later, exhausted and ruby-bottomed, Sally drifted off to a peaceful sleep, and Modan returned to the murky depths of her lake.

It had been a *very* educational day.

Chapter 8

The Spring

It was neither the singing of the birds nor the gentle caress of the rising sun that awoke Sally Vinebrook the following morning, but rather the heat and pressure of the water lapping around her legs and the weight of her body pulling at the vines around her arms and waist. With a yawn and an arching stretch of her back, she carefully started to open her eyes, allowing them time to adjust to the light as she tried to coax her still sleep-addled mind into figuring out what was going on.

She vaguely recalled Modan wrapping her in a vine harness and suspending her above the swamp to sleep once again after the previous night's activities, but something wasn't quite right about her current configuration. For starters, she wasn't *above* the lake anymore. Instead she was floating in the water up to her waist, the mostly-friendly vines gently swinging her by the shoulders and chest. Before she could deduce much more than that though, an involuntary shudder surged through her, and Sally's eyes bulged open in surprise as she felt something slick and insistent penetrate her.

"Eep!"

On instinct, she tried clamping her thighs around whatever it was that had snuck up between them, and felt a head of long, flowing hair pressed between them.

"Oh! M... Mistress... y-you, you... ahhhh..."

Starting to catch on to what was happening now, she *tried* to get her legs to relax and apologize, but the feeling of the naiad's tongue working its way in and out of her overrode her thoughts as it made her squirm in delight.

In response to her wriggling, Modan seized a buttock in each hand and squeezed possessively, seeming not to mind or perhaps even enjoy the pressure of the plump thighs around her head as she lapped at the inside of the girl's pussy and ground her lip up and down over her clitoris beneath the surface of the warm water.

Sally fluttered her legs from her knees downward in time with her mistress's lapping, her toes curling and uncurling with each increasingly frantic breath that bounced her naked breasts up and down above the lake. She wanted desperately to press herself even tighter against the water nymph now that she understood what was going on, to push her incredibly skilled tongue even deeper inside of her, but suspended as she was, all she could do was gasp and moan.

"P-please Mistress, don't stop!"

Modan continued to suck and lick and scourge relentlessly until Sally's body began to tremble and tighten, bare millimeters away from release. Then, with a gurgled laugh that sent tingling vibrations across the mage's overexcited lips, she forced her trembling legs apart and brought her head up to the surface, smiling tauntingly up at her from between her splayed thighs.

"Good morning, sweet one."

"G-good morning," panted Sally.

Seemingly of their own accord, her hips tried to wiggle closer to the naiad's tantalizingly close mouth in order to reach the climax they'd been promised, but the stupid vines holding her in place made that impossible, and all she managed to do was splash around like a struggling fish.

"Please!" she whimpered, arching her back to close the

distance.

"Mmmm?"

Modan looked up at her with wide, angelic eyes, feigning innocence.

Her smirk gave her away though.

"Please what?"

"Oooh," whined Sally, squirming her hips even more vigorously in an effort to draw attention to them. "I… I'm *so* close! Please, Mistress, j-just a little more!"

Modan nodded, though not in assent, just acknowledgement as she remained exactly where she was.

"Hmmm… No. I don't think so. You're awake now."

She let her grin widen by another couple of teeth.

"I've accomplished what I set out to do."

With a silent command from her, the vines then lowered the wriggling mage all the way into the murky water and released her, letting her sink down to her neck before floating back up again while they withdrew into the trees. Sally leveled a pout at Modan, but wisely decided not to push the issue any further just then. Although her fingers *did* start to wander down between her legs after she'd righted herself.

"Perhaps this way you'll be more motivated for today's lesson."

"Lesson, Mistress?" Sally asked, perking up from her sulking at the prospect of learning something new and exciting.

"What? Are you not interested in learning anything more? It hasn't quite been a few days yet, you know."

Modan snickered.

"And I wouldn't say that you've quite mastered all that you've attempted thus far. Although last night you certainly proved to be a far faster learner than I expected."

The memory of the previous night's "lesson" made Sally shiver and tingle all over again. On the one hand, she *had* managed to satisfy Modan, eventually. But on the other, it had taken no fewer than three more rounds of spanking before she got it exactly right!

The thought of her mistress's iron palm diverted Sally's wandering hands away from their journey between her thighs, and instead sent them zipping around to clamp onto her bottom. Shaking her head quickly from side to side in an effort to dissuade Modan of even the *hint* that she might be getting bored, she started babbling.

"No, no, no, Mistress! I do want to learn, I *do*!"

"I thought so."

Modan grinned toothily, victoriously even, at that; a conqueror gloating over a total subjugation.

"In that case, today I would like to show you more about the water and its minerals and their nature. And about the plants that spring and drink from it as well. There may be a small problem, though."

She paused then, looking about as close to concerned as Sally had seen her come so far.

"Can you shield yourself from being burned?"

"Burned?" echoed Sally, feeling her stomach flutter at the word as memories of the Kura's delights came flooding back unbidden in a hazy tangle that set her cheeks alight with a hot blush. "I um… I can definitely try if you're talking about pure heat, but if you're thinking about using those berries for something, I'm not so sure if I can…"

"Oooh, don't worry, sweet one."

Modan reached out and placed a comforting hand on Sally's cheek, encouraging her to rest her head against her palm.

"You'll get plenty more of Kura's delight in due time."

She smirked at the put-upon scowl this produced in her acolyte.

"However, I was referring to the hot spring at the center of the lake, where my mother's milk bubbles up from deep within earth. Can you protect yourself from the heat there?"

At the mention of the hot spring, Sally's face lit up with a smile as bright as the noon day sun.

"You're really going to show me the spring, Mistress?"

"I'd rather not repeat myself, unless you're ready to pay for it first thing in the morning."

Modan raised an eyebrow in mock-sternness then.

"Are you?"

Sally blushed and nuzzled the naiad's palm in reply to her question. She then chewed on her lower lip for a moment, looking up at her with big green eyes that contained a spark of mischief that hadn't been there a couple days earlier. Again, it was a tricky question to answer. So instead she tried picking a nice middle-of-the-road reply in the form of asking, "Um… So is that a yes?"

Modan's only answer was to grab her by the ear and start dragging her, with no regard for the pain or awkwardness as she pulled her sputtering through the water, over to the nearest available rock.

Even if the nymph's response *had* been the one she'd been (mostly) hoping for, being dragged by her ear toward a hard spanking was still an experience that Sally couldn't help but yelp and wriggle her way through.

"Please Mistress, I was just excited," she pleaded. "I didn't mean to be rude, it won't happen again!"

"I don't believe that for a second," scoffed Modan without deigning to look back at the mage as she hauled her up into the shallows, making her slosh desperately behind her to keep up. "And now you're lying to me as well. It seems you are determined to never, ever learn."

"No, really, I- Ah!"

Stopping abruptly, Modan plopped herself down onto a tall stone with a flat top jutting out from the muck and hoisted Sally into the air with her impressive strength before depositing her over her lap so that her head was hanging down just barely above the surface of the muddy, tadpole-swarming water. The tiny creatures stirring below the murk were interesting, but the curious little Cindertouched wasn't able to concentrate on them for very long as her mistress trapped her in place with an arm around her waist and launched into what must have been her ninth or tenth over-the-knee session since her arrival in her swamp.

SMACK! SMACK! SMACK!

The spanking itself wasn't nearly as hard as most of the previous ones had been. Instead, it was just a stern, painful reminder that relit the fires from the night before, and made Sally's aching sex groan even louder and more desperately for release.

—

The young mage's pussy wasn't the only thing that was aching when at last Modan was through with her. By the time the last swat had found its place and finished setting her bottom to jiggling, she was panting heavily and a light sheen of sweat had formed across her forehead and down the smooth valley of her arched back.

"I'm… I'm sorry… Mistress…" panted Sally between ragged breaths.

Once again, she was desperately close to the edge of climax, her hips wriggling across Modan's lap in search for something to rub against.

"I... I won't do it again, I promise."

"Good. I am totally convinced that you won't, and that I will not have to spank you a single other time for the duration of your stay."

"Humph!"

Modan smirked and gave Sally's bottom a few friendly pats, before casually pushing her forward off of her knees so that she belly-flopped into the muddy water in front of her with an undignified splash, laughing to herself at her splashing and sputtering.

"Now follow me to the spring, you naughty thing. You'll find some fruits and berries along the way."

Crawling back into the water without a second glance, she began to lead the way toward their destination, the top half of her head sticking out just above the surface and leaving a trail of floating hair behind her.

It took Sally a few moments of floundering in the shallows before she was able to once again reacquire her bearings, coughing and sputtering while attempting to pout at being denied her release yet again all at the same time. But soon she was scrambling off after the retreating dome of her mistress's head, stopping along the way to pluck a few fruits and berries from the various plants and trees as she splashed after her. She wasn't sure if the items she was gathering were supposed to be part of her lesson, or just her breakfast, so she made sure to gather a few extras just in case, nibbling on the sweet things along the way. After all, she didn't want to get in trouble again.

Well, at least not right away.

Modan set an easy pace for them as she led the way through the bog, past the cauldron trees and into the great clearing at its center where the bubbling pit was nestled amid the standing stones, sending its continuous plume of steam roiling up into the brilliant morning sky above. A light rain drizzled down around the edges of the island and the inner ring of the clearing, saturating the area with Power and life. A pair of large turtles could be seen floating idly around the lake, their heads sticking up on long necks to gaze dully around through the fog and steam, while smaller creatures splashed about and birds continued to sing from high above.

It was serene, yet undeniably primordial and thrumming with raw, untapped Power.

"Cast your spells and follow me," ordered Modan, as she glided on toward the central island nexus, around which the water fizzed and steamed in a low simmer.

Sally felt a knot of eager anticipation, and just a *little* bit of worry, form in the pit of her stomach as she watched her mistress drift away into the mist. On the one hand, as a Cin-dertouched, the spells to shield herself against heat and flame were among those that came most naturally to her., On the other… Failure in her spell-weaving here would *not* end well for her.

Gulping nervously, she paused near the edge of the boiling water and began to gather herself. Shaking her mop of damp, blonde locks to clear her head of any lingering doubts, she took her time inhaling deeply through her nose, holding the warm air within her lungs for a seven count, before exhaling it just as slowly through pursed lips.

"Alright Sally, you can do this."

Closing her eyes, she extended her perceptions out toward the unseen eddies and ethereal streams of the Power swirl-ing all around her. With an effort, she then began to draw those streams into her, wrapping them around herself and lashing them to her body's own aura as she began to recite the incantation for the enchantment that would prevent her from being burned to a crisp. As she worked her spell she felt a tingle, not unlike the one she'd experienced when her mistress had first kissed her, ripple over her skin as she intoned the words of Power for the third time, and when she finally opened her eyes a few moments later, she *knew* that she'd succeeded.

"Yes!"

Beaming brightly, joy and pride at having successfully cast the tricky spell radiating through her, Sally scrambled off to join Modan.

"I'm coming Mistress!"

Modan had already climbed up onto the crescent island and was waiting between the tall, geometric rocks lining it by the time Sally joined her. As the young mage splashed out of the shallows, she noticed that there were carvings etched into these strange stones as well, and that they were far more intact than the others she'd seen thus far. One depicted a woman with the face of a toad, the wings of a bat, and the tail of a fish, carved in a primitive and blocky style. Further down the moss covered column, beneath the toad-woman, were a circle of similarly crude, squat, humanlike figures with flat faces, long hair, and exaggerated chests and hips.

Modan smiled as Sally moved to stand in front of her.

"Good, you don't look burned. Well, most of you, at least."

She reached around and squeezed one of the mage's plump sit-spots at that, silently reminding her that she'd just been spanked. Although Sally's enchantment prevented her skin from being seared by the intense heat of the steaming island, it unfortunately did nothing to mitigate the warmth radiating from her naked rump. (If it had, she would've mastered it within her first month at the monastery!) So instead, she squirmed in her mistress's grip, and let out a half-nervous little giggle.

"This is where I was born," explained Modan, letting go of Sally's tush and gesturing toward the bubbling pit of mud at the island's center. "Or rather, where I was sent to grow up, depending on how you want to look at it."

Sally felt her eyes grow wide as saucers at this revelation, and, taking her hand off of the spot Modan had just squeezed, she eagerly swept her gaze around the small island again in the hope that she might see something from the naiad's childhood.

"Water nymphs don't play with toys do they?" she murmured to herself while absently chewing on her thumbnail as she squinted at the carvings, finding herself wishing that she'd brought some parchment and charcoal to make rubbings with.

"Oh, I play with toys."

Modan gave Sally a look that at once made her feel very, very uncomfortable, and simultaneously excited all at the same time. She then breezed past her over to the edge of the boiling hot spring and gestured down, the column of white steam shrieking up just in front of her breasts.

"I came up through here. I remember how it looked then. Dry. Red, barren hills everywhere."

She smiled wistfully, then.

"The grass and bushes grew soon after I came though, and the trees followed thereafter."

As she spoke, Sally couldn't help but stare in wide-eyed awe at all of the foliage and life that had developed since that time innumerable centuries ago. To think that where there was so much life now had once been barren and desolate?

Fascinating!

"This spring comes straight from my mother's cavern, you see. You'll find no more potent source of water anywhere on the surface world."

Modan gestured then for Sally to come join her.

"Now, try weaving an enchantment on it."

"R… right!"

Still reeling from what she'd just learned, the young mage approached the edge of the spring cautiously. While her spell kept its skin-searing heat at bay, the sheer amount of Power radiating off of it was overwhelming! Truth be told, it wasn't all that different from her mistress standing right next to her.

With another deep inhale and exhale, the steam merely tickling her lungs instead of flash-frying them thanks to her protective ward, she reached out with her mind and tried exerting her will on the water through the Power.

Come along now, water, don't be shy, she called to it, trying to coax some of it out of the bubbling pit.

To her delight and legitimate shock – this was definitely the realm of her Watertouched sisters, and most of her efforts were entirely guesswork now – a thin tendril did indeed coil up out of the gurgling mass, heeding her summons. However, maintaining control over it was a lot like trying to stay saddled on a wild stallion, and a moment later the tendril exploded. Sending boiling droplets of water out in all directions, and making Sally flinch and jump back in surprise.

"Ah! Oh… oh my," she breathed, laughing nervously and peering back at the spring with a newfound respect.

"It still remembers my mother," explained Modan. "Still knows that it's alive. You can't just command it, you need to appease it. Convince it that you are *worthy* of shaping it."

She took a step back then and watched the naked, red-bottomed girl standing before the spring with an enigmatic smirk.

"See if you can manage something."

"Convince it?" repeated Sally, eyeing the bubbling spring

dubiously as she tried to figure out what she could possibly do to convince countless gallons of boiling water that she was worth listening to.

Part of her wanted to just ask how she should do that, but the greater part of her wanted to puzzle it out on her own and impress her mistress. Hoping that maybe there was something she'd overlooked, she squinted at the carvings on the stones again, but those didn't seem to offer any answers.

Oh well, I suppose I may as well try again…

Closing her eyes, she extended her hands out toward the spring. Maybe if she set aside her mundane sight altogether she'd be able to see what she should do? With another breath, she reached out once again and drew her ethereal presence up to its full stature, putting out another thought with a bit more emphasis this time and prefacing it with more elaborate words of Power.

Um… Hello, Mistress Water. My name is Sally Vinebrook. I know you're busy helping everything around here grow, but would you mind lending me some of your Power for just a little bit?

With that mental request, she once again formed the thought of coaxing a tendril of water up and out, trying to show the hot spring what exactly she was trying to do, and hoping that it would agree to help.

And once again it appeared to work.

For a moment, anyway.

Her water-knot quickly exploded again almost as soon as it had formed, this time with even greater violence, and Modan shook her flower-strewn head.

"You cannot wheedle this spring, nor can you overpower it."

Stepping closer, she put a hand under Sally's chin and

turned her head up, tipping it back so that she was forced to look her in the eye.

"What do you know of this spring? Of its personality?" she pressed.

"J-just what you've told me Mistress," replied Sally, trying to keep the disappointment and nervousness out of her voice. "You said it remembers your mother and that it's willful. So I just thought that maybe if I was nicer to it…"

Modan pursed her lips and shook her head again.

"Is being nice enough? Tell me about this spring. Tell me what it desires, what pleases it, and what must be done for it to *want* to help you."

Sally pursed her own lips and furrowed her brow in concentration as she tried to puzzle out the naiad's words.

"What it desires…" she murmured softly, rolling the words around her tongue, as if tasting them might yield some fresh insight.

"Well, I know that the spring stems from your mother's cavern, from the river goddess Arthun's cavern," she continued, spooling out her thoughts like twine as she worked her way toward a conclusion. "If it comes from the river goddess's cavern, then it would definitely obey one of her children, but I'm not one of those, so… Hmmm…"

Frowning, she looked at her mistress with concern and asked, "Is it ability that it craves? Am I not strong enough for it to think me worthy of obeying, Mistress?"

In response, Modan shifted around to stand behind Sally, and put a hand on each of her shoulders, gently squeezing and massaging. Suddenly, she brought her face forward and bit the crook of the girl's neck. Not hard at first, just slowly bringing her teeth together and pulling at her skin. She let go after a moment, and then gave her another bite, this time on her ear, and ran her tongue-tip *very* gently along its inner rim, asking again, "What do you know about this spring? What have you learned about it?"

Her mistress's nibbles and bites raised the temperature in Sally's face to something approaching that of the spring itself. Her face started to glow nearly as red as her bottom, and for a few moments all she could do was fumble around for words. After what felt like forever to her, but couldn't actually have been more than a few seconds, she managed to regain enough control of her tongue to offer up hopefully, "It um… It's the base from which all the life in the bog draws its strength? That from the smallest crawler to the biggest knucker, and all the plants in between, that they all carry some part of it?"

"Yes," Modan whispered into her ear. "But you are forgetting something even more basic. Something you already know."

Snaking an arm around the mage, she pinched her left nipple, rolling it between her fingers and using the rest of her hand to grope and squeeze at her breast. While she did that, her other hand slid down along the water-slicked skin of her stomach, before gripping her between her legs and yanking her back so that her hot bottom was scratched by the thatch of dark hair at her mistress's groin and her arched back was pressed against the ample swell of her breasts.

"Ah! M-Mistress…!" Sally moaned, overcome by sensation all at once.

Ignoring her feeble struggles, Modan murmured against her ear again, louder and with more force this time.

"Everything has a spirit, little human. Every rock. Every stream. Every hill."

She bit Sally's earlobe again, harder.

"Who is the spirit of this spring, and what earns her

cooperation?"

Sally squirmed in her mistress's arms, caught once again in the contradictory void of pain and pleasure that she just couldn't seem to stay out of, as she tried desperately to focus on her words even as her body reacted to her touches.

"A-Arthun!" she cried out, her lower lip trembling as she hovered only steps away from the precipice of release.

Modan's voice was an actual growl now.

"No!"

She pushed Sally forward, forcing her down onto her knees as both hands seized hold of her breasts in a painful squeeze and her mouth yanked at her hair.

"*I* am the spirit of the misty bog. *I* am the life of the boiling spring. My mother is deep and far below us. This spring is *me*! What you see before you now is my true body!"

Modan pinched each nipple *hard* and gave them a merciless twist that had Sally arching her back with a cry of pain, before then moving her hands up to the mage's shoulders, shoving her forward and making her bow down.

"What pleases me? What have you done that earns my favor?"

"Ack! Oh! Mistress please, I'm sorry!" cried Sally, her body absorbing the naiad's displeasure like a sponge even as her hips rose up higher to accept whatever else she might deem necessary.

It really *was* pretty obvious in hindsight, she had to admit. Of course this was her bog! Part of her wanted to protest that it wasn't her fault, that she would have answered correctly had she not been so... distracted, but it was only a fleeting thought that burst and dissipated almost as quickly as one of the bubbles in the spring before her.

"Please don't be upset with me, Mistress!" she moaned

instead, genuine fear and worry that she'd upset Modan seeping into her cry. "I-I… wish only to obey and learn from you. I will do whatever you command!"

"Yes. Yes you will."

Modan thrust her big hips into Sally's sore bottom, making it sting anew as she ground herself hard against her tender skin.

"Tell me what commands you will obey."

She then reached out and grabbed a handful of honey blonde hair, yanking the girl's head upward and jerking her gaze away from the boiling mud to the steam that rose from it.

"W-whatever you desire, Mistress," she gasped out, her sore and stinging buttocks wriggling against her mistress's warm hips seemingly of their own accord as her breath started coming in ragged pants. "S-simply name it, and I will obey!"

"Now."

Modan rose to her feet, hauling Sally up with her and gripping her hair in one hand and her throat in the other as her mouth continued growling and tonguing at her ear.

"Cast. Your. Spell."

"Oh horsefeathers!" the girl moaned, completely undone by the naiad's harsh order.

It was one thing to make promises, but another thing entirely to have to actually carry them out. Still though, her mistress *had* commanded it, and she *had* promised to obey, and by all the gods below and above she was sure as the moon going to try! She squirmed with the effort of trying to focus, doing her best to ignore the twinge of panic her oath produced in her (not to mention the hands around her throat and hair!) With a supreme effort of will, she reached out once again to the bubbling cauldron in front of her and cried aloud,

"Come to me! In the name of your mistress and mine, Modan, daughter of Arthun, I call you to obey!"

The steam condensed as it rose from the bubbling mud, forming itself into a watery likeness of Sally Vinebrook, naked and flushed and open mouthed. Unlike the mere flickers and small movements she'd managed to conjure before, this elemental actually strode forth onto the land, maintaining itself and obeying her mental commands until, overwhelmed with what she'd just done, she let it collapse into a shower of droplets and steam.

A coherent water elemental! I can't even do that with stone or fire yet!

Modan barely gave her enough time to appreciate what she'd just done however, before slamming her face and chest back down into the mud, bearing down on her. Quick as a striking water snake, she slipped one hand around her front and began to attack her pussy lips, firmly stroking and sliding them around.

"That is correct. The Power here will heed you, provided you worship it. Worship *me*."

With a haughty sneer, the naiad pressed the mage's cheek even further into the mud and ground her crotch into her sore ass as she continued stroking and groping between her lower lips, slowly working one finger and then two inside of her.

"Ah!"

Euphoria, both from successfully summoning a fully formed water elemental for the first time, and from her mistress's fingers working their way deeper and deeper into her as if to illustrate how utterly and completely she belonged to her, bubbled up inside of Sally until it was roiling and boiling like the waters of the spring in front of her.

"Mistress!" she cried out, drawing the single word out even

as the mud half-muffled it.

That single word containing all of her feelings of devotion and obedience.

A special hymn, a prayer for only her that only she could offer.

"Speak, and I will obey!"

"Alright."

Modan giggled almost innocently then, her earlier primal fury seeming to have completely dissipated as she released the mage without any warning and stood up.

"Roam the bog, and see what else you can do now that you understand the nature of the water. Then meet me in the tree where we played yesterday when the first frogs begin to croak this evening."

"Y-yes, ma'am," panted Sally, still lying face down in the mud as her trembling hands desperately sought the juncture between her thighs, hoping to somehow finish herself off before the moment passed her by.

Noticing this, Modan bent forward and swatted the prostrate girl's jiggly bottom one last time.

SMACK!

"And don't you *dare* touch yourself until then."

With that, she then nonchalantly strode back into the water, leaving Sally to groan in frustration as she clenched her fists impotently in the mud.

It was going to be a long, *long* afternoon.

Chapter 9

Practice Makes Perfect

When the croak of the first frog finally came, signaling with it the fall of evening, Sally Vinebrook sprang to her feet from where she'd been sitting cross-legged in the mud at the edge of the ruin island near the bubbling spring and all but dove into the murky lake behind her, making a beeline toward the tree where she'd had her lesson in "serving" her mistress the previous evening. Pumping her legs vigorously, she reached the trunk nearly out of breath, but in record time. She was becoming a far better swimmer just in these last few days.

Climbing up onto one of the tree's slick, moss-covered roots, she stumbled forward a few steps and plopped her back against its gnarled trunk and tried to catch her breath. As she did so, she cast a contemplative look up into the thick canopy above her, wondering with some trepidation how it was that she was going to get up there. For a moment she considered trying to climb the tree, but quickly tossed that idea aside. She didn't have the skill for something like that, especially with her arms already tired from swimming, and besides, the nearest handholds she could see were more than two meters above her head.

"No choice, I suppose…"

Fidgeting nervously, she let out a long, protracted sigh, and then reached out with her mind to touch the creepers hanging throughout the canopy.

Excuse me, I need to get up there to join our mistress, will you please help me up?

She finished with the proper arcane syntax, whispered aloud. In response to her call, several vines slithered down from the branches high above. They then looped themselves around and under each of her armpits and began to haul her up. As they did so, Sally could feel the same sense of smugness and mockery they'd been exuding ever since assisting Modan with her discipline that very first evening when she'd arrived, and she couldn't help but get the impression that they were squeezing around her shoulders and back just a little tighter than was strictly necessary.

She endured all of this with merely a pouty huff however, thinking and saying nothing that might insult the surprisingly sensitive plants, and eventually she found herself dangling amid a mass of algae and moss-hung branches crawling with vines several meters above the surface of the water below. A soft, cool drizzle was falling down through the light foliage above and it sprinkled against her skin, contrasting shockingly with the warm mist all around her as she remained there, hanging.

At first she waited patiently for the vines to release their snug hold from around her armpits so that she could drop down onto the branch just beneath her feet, but after several long seconds it grew apparent that they had no intention of letting go. Which was exactly what she'd been afraid of.

Gritting her teeth, Sally wriggled in the vine's grip, squirming her legs and arms around in a vain attempt to try and slip free from them on her own.

Alright, you can let me go now, she thought at the creepers, trying not to let them pick up on the embarrassment and worry slowly starting to edge its way into her perception. *Thank you for all of your help, but I can take it from here!*

"Mmmm… Such a lovely decoration. I'm half-tempted to keep you there," purred a melodious voice in greeting from somewhere behind her, making Sally squeak in surprise. "Wouldn't that be lovely? A beautiful human girl hanging in the trees for all who pass through to see and admire? Like a flower or a luscious fruit."

Sally's entire body began to glow a hot pink, and her struggles intensified three-fold as visions of total strangers riding through the forest ogling her naked, suspended, and helpless for their viewing pleasure appeared before her mind's eye. It was one thing to be left to stand outside the monastery refectory with a well-spanked bare bottom on display as an object lesson to her fellow sisters, but this would be something else entirely!

"Nooo," she moaned, even as her thighs squeezed together at the thought of how deliciously embarrassing that would be. "Please Mistress, I can't!"

"Oh, I think that you can."

With a silent command from Modan, the vines began to rearrange themselves around Sally. Others swooped in to grasp the wriggling mage as the first ones let her go, causing her to swing gently from side to side as she was repositioned just above a platform of thickly knotted and overgrown branches off to her right.

She could feel the naiad's body heat radiating out from just behind her, and she shivered with anxious anticipation as she felt the naiad touch her shoulder blade, running a single, totally in control fingertip down along the column of her spine to the small of her back.

"Surely you can deal with some unruly arch vines, now that you're a green wizardess who has plumbed the depths of their swamp for nearly three whole days?"

Modan chuckled darkly.

"Of course, the longer it takes you to get free of them, the more likely it is that the lady of this place will grow bored merely watching. And then she will have to *amuse* herself."

Another vine descended from somewhere above them then, snaking around Sally's waist, and the three of them hoisted her up a few inches higher. This caused Modan's finger to be dragged along the upper curve of her bottom until it was poking her right in the sit-spot, just above her empowered signature. Despite the precariousness of Sally's predicament, the sensation of her mistress's fingertip tickling her sensitive cheek and sit-spot made her giggle. Which in turn made her squirm, making her giggle all the more.

"So…"

Modan patted her a few times, keeping her voice tauntingly nonchalant.

"You should probably give it an earnest try."

Sally could feel the vines holding her chuckling right along with the naiad, which caused her to blush even deeper and pout tremendously as she reached out desperately to them once again.

Let me go, let me go!

The vines only tightened their grip however, and the one around her belly pulled itself slightly upward, raising her bottom and legs as it forced her to arch her back.

Grinning hungrily, Modan seized the opportunity being presented to her and delivered a sharp slap to the center of first one cheek, and then the other.

SMACK! SMACK!

"We're off to rather a bad start, aren't we, sweet one?"

She then gave each cheek another, harder slap, making sure each one *really* packed a wallop this time.

SMACK! SMACK!

"Oh! Ack! Ow, owie!"

Sally squirmed in her vine harness, fluttering her legs behind her as if somehow she could swim through the air and escape the clinging creepers and her mistress's casual bottom swats.

"T-they won't listen to me!" she whined impetuously.

Squeezing her eyes shut tight, she resumed trying to get the vines to let her go, alternating between pleading and threatening all sorts of horrible fates, that due to her genuinely kind nature amounted to little more than minor inconveniences at best. The vines just laughed and tightened their grip on her however, content to side with Modan instead of her as they abstractly communicated how much they enjoyed "helping" her mistress.

"Come now," chided the naiad. "Surely you can do better than that. Or at least, I hope you can."

Modan paused for a moment.

"Or do I?"

As if in response to her rhetorical question, the vine around Sally's waist pulled up higher still, so that her rear end was angled just above her head, which was now hanging roughly around the level of her parted knees. With this change in position came a new perspective for her as well, and she huffed out an indignant pout as she caught sight of Modan standing on a thick branch behind her, grinning.

Making eye contact with her trapped student, the naiad drew half a step closer and reached out to slide her left hand between her soft cheeks. She then used her fingers to spread them open, and began to deliver a series of ruthless, wrist-flicking swats to the inside of her cleft.

SLAP-SMACK! SLAP-SMACK! SLAP-SMACK!

Sally let out a long, high-pitched squeal of agony and pulled her balled up fists in tight against her swaying chest as she felt her mistress begin to light a fire in one of her most tender areas.

Ignoring Sally's cries, andgiggling and chortling all the while as she went, Modan swatted away at the insides of both buttocks, where pain was never meant to be experienced.

"Or maybe I really *will* have a new decoration? A shiny, red, weeping decoration."

As Modan swatted away seemingly without a care in the world, Sally tried desperately to clench her bottom cheeks together, to shield their inner cleft from Modan's casual abuse, but her fingers were like a steel vice prying them apart, and she was left with no other choice but to weep and cry out.

"Pleeeeease Mistress, pleeease! They won't listen to me! Please don't leave me up here like this, it's too embarrassing!"

"Don't talk to *me*, sweet. It's the arch vines you must deal with. I'm simply taking innocent advantage of the, shall we say…"

Grinning wickedly, Modan paused long enough to lean forward and run her tongue along the length of the exposed area between Sally's cheeks, making the girl shiver and gasp and savoring the heat she tasted there, before drawing back and resuming her attack on a now freshly wetted target.

"…'S*ituation*' right in front of me."

SLAP-SMACK! SLAP-SMACK! SLAP-SMACK!

Humming quietly to herself, she swatted the inside of each cheek five more times, very fast and *very* hard, and then once more directly over Sally's delightfully puckered anus, making her shriek loud enough to send birds scattering from their nests in the distance.

"Oh gods below, that *stings*!"

Panting and sweating, Sally was relieved beyond words when Modan at last let her cheeks ease back together. But that relief just as quickly turned to horror as the vines around her head and arms lowered her torso even further so that she was nearly upside down, and her stomach lurched as she saw her mistress wrapping another, thinner vine around her arm like she had two days prior.

"Come now, surely you can solve this one silly, little puzzle?"

Modan reached out and let the tendril coiled around her right forearm rub itself hungrily across both of Sally's cheeks, before then raising her arm up with a cruel grin and lashing her across both sit-spots at once.

THWACK!

"I'm trying!" squealed Sally, kicking her feet forward and back in a frantic attempt to run away from the vine whip, which merely made her sway in her restraints. "Really Mistress, I am!"

"What is it that wise bog mystics say again?" taunted Modan in turn. "Hmmm… Oh yes, that's right. 'Do or do not, there is no try'."

She laughed at that and then brought down her lash again, and again, leaving two more lines across both of the mage's cheeks.

THWACK! THWACK!

Screwing her eyes shut tight, Sally gritted her teeth and focused on the vines, projecting with as much ferocity as she could the image of them uncoiling from around her.

Listen, blast you! I'm serious! Let me go, let me goooo!

At her impassioned command, the vines around her arms began to loosen, and the one around her waist started to tremble, as if shuddering in fear. However, a moment later, they redoubled their grip, and another loop descended from above to ensnare her ankles, squeezing tight.

"Uh-uh-uh," chided Modan with a disapproving cluck of her tongue before she whipped her again.

THWACK!

And again.

THWACK!

And then again, against the tops of her thighs this time.

THWACK-THWACK!

"Aieee!"

"Brute force isn't the answer, dear."

She whipped the mage yet again, and laughed once more.

THWACK!

"Try again."

Great fat teardrops were dribbling down Sally's face now, tracing along her delicate jawline and falling below to feed the trees, and as Modan intensified her lashing, all she was able to do was wriggle and cry.

"I *am* trying!"

THWACK!

"You'd better try harder then."

Gathering herself again, she gave a great, heaving sniffle and let out a long, shaky breath. With a supreme effort of will, Sally did her best to shut out the lines of fire being burned across her cheeks and focused her mind on the Power and the vines now squeezing tighter than ever around her.

Please release me, vines. In the name of our Mistress, I'm asking you to release me!

Then, deciding it couldn't hurt to try, she added with a hopeful smile.

Pretty please?

With that, the vines clinging to her immediately began to draw back like snakes slithering up into the canopy, uncoiling and dropping away from her armpits and ankles, and breaking out from under her waist all at once. Immediately, Sally dropped into a deadfall, but half a heartbeat later she came to an abrupt halt as a fresh pair of vines snatched her by the ankles, and another one lashed out to cushion her head from the recoil.

"Not bad. But that could have been problematic had I not commanded these others to catch you," observed Modan as she descended from above through the steeple of branches, raindrops, and mist, supported by a pair of vine tendrils of her own. "You'll have to think one or two more steps in advance, sweet."

Her voice was rich and melodious as she came to a stop just above Sally and delivered another vertical lash along the girl's left cheek from right behind her, and then another on her right.

THWACK-THWACK!

"Aieee! Yes Mistress!" squealed Sally in reply, wriggling in an ineffectual attempt to escape her mistress's punishing displeasure.

On reflex, her right hand flew back to hover over her bottom as she tried to decide if she should chance a rub or not, while her left remained firmly wrapped in a loose fist around the prize of her labors from that afternoon, cradling it against her chest protectively.

"I-I'll remember that for next time, I promise!"

Modan used the girl's moment of indecision as an opportunity to whip another, thinner, vine around her right wrist, yanking it off to the side, and then following it up with three more lashes across her inverted bum.

THWACK! THWACK! THWACK!

"Well, for starters, it looks like you need to get free once again."

THWACK!

"And I think you've learned by now what happens when I need to save you from falling."

Modan then had the vines pull on Sally so that she was lying face up, back horizontal, and ankles hoisted straight in the air to offer her tautly-stretched bottom and thighs to her. With a low chuckle, she perched herself with preternatural grace on another slimy branch just below her, and with her deep black eyes glistening, whipped the lash again and again and again.

With her feet trapped in the air above her, all Sally could do was try and wiggle her hips from side to side, moaning and yelping and promising to do better as searing lash after searing lash took bite after bite of her rapidly reddening and welting flesh. As tears streaked down her face and her breasts heaved freely with each ragged breath, she tried picturing the vines loosening their grip around her ankles, but instead of just letting her fall free, she tried to communicate to them the idea that she wanted them to *slowly* lower her legs and then the rest of her body down onto the branch below.

"Please!" she cried aloud, no longer sure if she was begging her mistress to stop, or the vines to obey.

"You had it before. Now you're going back to something that you *know* doesn't work." admonished Modan with a shake of her head and a mocking smile, doing a surprisingly good job of approximating the tone of one of Sally's sterner instructors from the monastery.

"Oh, what's this?"

She sounded totally different then, innocently excited as she took her eyes off of the welted tush in front of her and beamed at something on the branch beside her.

"Why those are some Kura's delights! Oh, how perfect!"

With a cruel giggle, Modan straightened up again with a pair of plump red berries in each hand. Crushing them into pulp between her fists, she then slowly advanced on the trapped mage while grinning from ear to ear.

"No hurry now. Take your time and figure this one out, dear."

Sally felt the color drain out of her face and her stomach ball itself up into an icy knot as her mistress began kneading the deceptively cool pulp onto her fresh welts and in between her reddened cheeks, humming pleasantly to herself as she worked. But even though she knew what was going to start happening to her in just a few short moments, the sensation of the naiad's strong hands massaging the cool juice into her sore skin *did* feel good, and a soft sigh escaped her lips.

"Ahhh…"

Then, remembering that she was on a short fuse before the *real* inferno touched off in her backside, she began frantically racking her mind for whatever it was that she'd done the last time to make the darn vines obey.

"Oh no, oh no, oh my, oh no, no, no, no, no!" she began to chant as her heart rate skyrocketed. "Please Mistress, no, no, noooooo!"

"Keep begging me for mercy, please. I'm sure you'll sway me eventually."

With half a thought, Modan ordered the vines to part Sally's ankles, spreading her legs out to either side and offering the girl's sopping wet vagina to her.

"Oh gods…"

In an effort to help her clear her mind and concentrate entirely on the problem at hand that needed solving, Modan bit her lower lip and flashed her a pair of smoldering bedroom eyes between her parted legs, before then bending forward to blow cool air across her swollen, sensitive lips.

"Time runs short, sweet thing…"

She bit her lip again then, licking it lasciviously, before leaning forward and sticking her tongue all the way out to massage it up and down along the length of the mage's labia, pausing every now and again to swivel it around her clitoris. Meanwhile, her hands came up to cup either bum cheek, squeezing them gently and coaxing the berry juice there to start to burn and flame the quivering girl's tender skin.

"Haaah… haaah… oooooh…" moaned Sally, the noises escaping her in low, guttural purrs.

She hadn't realized just how wet her mistress had been making her all throughout this whole ordeal, and with her legs now parted, her spine desperately lifted her hips up as high as she could manage. Trying simultaneously to receive more of Modan's oral attention, while at the same time escape the rapidly mounting berry-heat as it radiated in faster and faster waves off of her red and welted bottom.

Horsefeathers and dragon spit! she cursed silently to herself as she gnawed on her lower lip, her eyes rolling up in a heady mixture of pleasure and pain. *How are her hands not burning right now? Is it because she's a water nymph?*

Seemingly in taunting response to her racing thoughts, Modan moved her hands away from Sally's buttocks and grabbed her thighs instead, forcing them further apart and bringing her face in to lap at her closer, and more deeply, sending a shiver and spasm through the gasping girl with each lick. Meanwhile, another vine rose up from below, and began following up each of her licks with one of its own, across one cheek and then the other.

THWACK! THWACK! THWACK!

Making the burning berry juice positively *explode*!

"Aieee!"

Sally's eyes shot open wide and nearly bulged out of her head entirely as the treacherous vine joined in on the licking, and her cries ratcheted up several more octaves until they became one continuous, high-pitched wail of agonized ecstasy that echoed across the canopy for the entire bog to hear.

"*Please* Mistress!" she all but sobbed, her words tumbling out of her like rocks down a hill. "I… I can't take it anymore! I'm going to… I'm going to!"

Gritting her teeth and squeezing her eyes shut tight, she tried desperately to fumble her way back to the vines, but her mind was a tumultuous sea where no focused thought could find sure footing, and in moments she was swallowed up into it.

"Oh… oh! Oh gods!"

Pulling back, Modan just shook her head and sighed, rolling her eyes in mock-exasperation.

"Silly thing."

Removing her face from Sally's groin, she picked up something else. A round, soft bit of wood, about as long as her finger and slightly thicker, with depressed rings worn into and around its smooth length. Still grinning, she crushed a few more berries across its length, and then, just as the mage was beginning to get her bearings again, pushed its tip up against her little bottom hole, spreading her cheeks wide with the fingers of her other hand to make room for it.

"Huh? Whassat?" slurred a still dreamy Sally, putting only the barest minimum amount of effort into trying to squirm away as she felt her mistress start to penetrate her from behind.

The sticky, wet berry juices helped the rigid, curvy thing

AshleyOTK

slide nearly all the way inside of her with barely any resistance, and Modan giggled as it sank up to the final ridge near its base.

"Only you can save yourself, sweetness."

With those ominous words and a fond pat against the base of her newly-inserted toy, she returned her tongue to the girl's pussy, and the vines resumed their whipping in tiny, not too hard strokes against each of her sit-spots. Swatting lazily, knowing that they didn't have to do it any harder than that to get the desired reaction.

THWIP. THWIP. THWIP.

Sally's cheeks were already on fire, but this new sensation assailing her *insides* was something else entirely! On reflex, her anus clamped down around the base of the wooden plug as it began to sizzle within her, which proved to be a *huge* mistake.

Tossing her head back as a newfound panic took hold of her heart and squeezed it mercilessly, she howled as the berry juice coating the knobbly peg turned the ultra-sensitive inner tissue of her bottom to boiling magma. The heat soaking into her flesh made her thrash and kick her legs, which jerked her little hole even more roughly around the plug, which in turn ratcheted up the heat as a result!

"Oh gods!"

Truly, it was an *exquisite* agony, and the young mage screamed and thrashed her head from side to side, pain exploding both inside and outside of her bottom and colliding with the huge tidal waves of pleasure rippling outward from where the naiad's tongue was relentlessly plumbing and massaging her aching core.

"Mistress! Oh gods, it stings so much, please!"

Her cries fell on deaf ears however, and Sally was only

peripherally aware of what was happening around her now as the vines wrapped around her pulled her right-side-up, and the tongue lapping at her womanhood was replaced by another wet – but rounder and rougher – lashing thing.

You stupid vines. That is not what I meant when I asked you to help me! she thought with a mental snarl, before just as quickly changing her mind as the writhing tendril got to work in earnest. *Oh… N-never mind, c… carry on…*

However the boiling in her bottom and the teasing at her slit were soon supplanted by the new sensations of teeth and fingers rolling around each of her nipples, hands cupping under her breasts, and a mouth shifting from one to the other, sucking on each rock hard tip as if desperate for milk.

"Focus," chided Modan in false-sternness, chuckling against the nipple she had clamped between her teeth before flicking her tongue against it.

Sally didn't bother with replying this time, other than to cry out again in agonized ecstasy.

As she writhed, the rain continued to fall, the mist warmed, the plug burned, one vine whipped, one rubbed, and hands and mouth tortured her breasts. After several long and excruciatingly wonderful moments of this, the vine teasing at her folds pulled back, and then without any warning snaked its way inside of her, gyrating in and out while simultaneously wriggling like a worm or snake.

"Ah!"

When the vine penetrated her, Sally's mouth and eyes shot wide open, and she gasped. In spite of the pain in her bottom, a low laugh of pure erotic pleasure bubbled up and out of her, and her knees wiggled in a desperate search for support that just wasn't there.

"M-Mistress!" she gasped between her yelps and moans,

looking down and searching desperately for the naiad's inky eyes, feeling a sudden panic seizing hold of her that if she couldn't cling to her gaze as an anchor, then she would be lost in a sea of pain and pleasure forever. "Mistress, *please*!"

Modan wasn't going to let her off the hook (or in this case vine) so easily though, and silenced her pleading by removing her mouth from the girl's breasts and bringing it up to meet hers, holding her head firmly in place with both hands to quell her frenzied thrashing and struggling. Her massed tears didn't bother her in the slightest as they kissed, and at her mental command, the vine inside of Sally started pumping harder and faster than ever, taking her with reckless, primal abandon that drove her wild.

Pulling her mouth away, Modan licked at her lips and let her face hover mere inches away from Sally's, just out of reach, and watched the mage suffer with an expression of pure, merciless lust.

The look in her mistress's eyes coupled with the feverish pumping of the vine conspired together to push Sally dangerously close to the edge again, but something inside of her made her hold back from tipping over just yet. Locking her gaze with Modan's, she silently pleaded for release, even as her bottom reflexively continued to clench and unclench in time with the whipping vines.

Please!

Instead of granting her wish however, Modan just let the vines whipping and pumping fall away, and straightened back up to pull the plug out of her bottom. She massaged both of her thoroughly reddened cheeks a bit, then, as she purred quietly, "Perhaps I've been too hard on you? Alright, I'll give you a break."

With a snap of her fingers, the vines wrapped around Sally's ankles retracted up toward the canopy again, pulling her higher and drawing her back into a more relaxed position with her round, red cheeks right in front of the naiad's smiling lips.

In front of and below her, Modan reached out and spread Sally's cheeks yet again, and looking her shamelessly in the eye between her parted thighs, stuck her tongue into her open back door. Pushing it in as far as it would go, she kept her eyes locked on the mage's, as she tried to clean away as much of the burning berry juice as she could.

A serene, dreamy smile spread across Sally's lips then, even as her face flushed a hot crimson. In spite of her embarrassment, she forced herself to keep her eyes locked on her mistress's as her tongue probed and plunged in and out of her in a way that very clearly communicated that she belonged to her in every sense of the word. Her warm, slick tongue felt absolutely *amazing*, especially after the hell that had been the fireroot, and her sobs and sniffles soon were replaced by more shallow gasps and low moans of pleasure.

She was *so* tantalizingly close to climaxing now, but she forced herself to hold back still, to demonstrate her willingness to obey the Lady of the Mist completely as she waited with rapidly mounting impatience for her approval to come.

Sometime much, *much* later, Modan at last pulled her face back and licked her lips clean.

"I can't really say you've impressed me with your mastery of the Power, or of the bog."

She lowered her eyelids and sighed.

"And yet, I can't bring myself to be angry."

Falling backwards, she let herself be caught up in a net of vines with her legs splayed open, her slick vulva and huge, round buttocks exposed to the mage in a mirror of her own pose. The vines holding Sally then lowered her onto the branch where she'd just been standing, and she smiled at the girl imperiously.

"So I'll just have to have you demonstrate something else for me instead. Now, girl. I command you to fuck me."

Sally snapped to attention at the order, the brusqueness of it and the casual way her mistress was lounging back awaiting her obedience making her whole body flush with heart-pounding exceitment.

"Y-yes, Mistress!"

Dropping to her knees on the branch, she tentatively scooted her way forward so that she was kneeling between Modan's parted thighs and staring up at her glistening sex. With a nervous smile, she leaned forward, her head hovering uncertainly between moving to her groin or up to attend to her breasts.

"W-with my m-mouth, Mistress?"

Quick as a flash, the vines supporting Modan pulled her up into a sitting position, so that she was perched in a swing made from them, and seizing Sally by the arm and hair, she yanked her over her lap, hauling her up so that her legs dangled freely over one side and her torso and head were held aloft by vines on the other.

Leaning into the girl's back, digging her elbow in hard between her shoulder blades, she growled, "When I tell you to do something, you do *not* ask questions, you instead *do* it!"

She then launched straight into another full force, open-handed, bare bottom spanking that echoed across the canopy and over the bog, striking mercilessly atop Sally's already striped and still berry-burned seat.

SMACK! SMACK! SMACK!

Her arm moving in a blur, Modan's palm danced a circle around each cheek in turn, causing them to wobble and ripple as furiously as the muddy water of her hot spring.

"Mistress! I didn't- Oh! I was- Ah! I won- owww!" Sally started to sob, excuses, apologies, and explanations all tumbling over each other in a stampede to flee her mouth as a firestorm of agony was rained down upon her poor, burning bottom.

She wept across Modan's lap and quietly hoped that she wouldn't be too upset with her, and that she would have another chance to satisfy her, silently berating herself for being so foolish and not doing as she'd been told.

"Please Mistress, forgive meeee!"

Modan didn't reply, but simply spanked. The very image of a curvaceous, wild goddess, disciplining a crying and struggling (and also quite curvaceous) girl over her lap. No mercy. No mockery. Just a spanking, because she wanted to give one, and didn't want to hold back.

SMACK! SMACK! SMACK!

—

By the time it was finally over, Sally's bottom had swollen to half again its already impressive natural size, and was well on its way toward a striking shade of purple.

Modan smiled as she slowed her swatting and then stopped entirely, petting the flesh she'd just ruined.

"Poor, poor, sweet girl," she cooed smugly.

She then lowered the two of them slowly to just above the water, and grabbed some honeyberries to rub in against the targets of her displeasure.

"You need to work on recalling your lessons, sweet. I taught you the magic of the bog, and I taught you how to delight a woman. You know both. I know you remember it all."

With surprising gentleness, she began kneading the soothing berries into scalded flesh, rubbing the mage's pussy in between bouts of gentle massaging elsewhere.

"But you must learn to think quickly. Recall it when needed at a moment's notice."

She smiled viciously then as a delightful idea came to her and she immediately switched gears.

"And to prove to me that you're taking this much-needed lesson to heart, you're going to come on my lap right now before I let you up. Be quick about it, though, or else it's another switching."

With that dire warning, she let one finger probe into Sally as the other continued its aftercare.

Sally, who had been sniffling and shuddering in equal measures as the wonderful berries were applied to her battered and beaten bottom, started to giggle uncontrollably.

Finally! An order she could carry out without even a shadow of self-doubt.

"Y-yes Mistress, thank you, Mistress!" she gasped out between laughs, before letting out a long, low cry of delight and letting herself go, surrendering fully to Modan's skilled hands entirely.

Some minutes later the walls of her sex clamped down in rhythmic contractions around the naiad's thrusting finger, as if embracing it tightly and promising to never let it go, and bright white stars flashed behind her eyes.

"Oh! Oh gods, ahhh!"

She rode the waves of her climax for what felt like forever, and by the time she was carried back to the shores of reality, she was laying like a limp sack of potatoes across her mistress's knees, practically drooling. By some small miracle though, her hands still clung protectively around the fruits of her labor from the day's lesson, and with a smile, she nestled it tightly into her chest and giggled again.

"Tomorrow you may recover," said Modan as she petted and kissed and simply loved the girl over her lap. "The next day I will test you again, and you will do better then."

She idly played with her hair for a little longer then, before at last tipping Sally's head around to kiss her on the mouth, this time letting her tongue dive deep inside to fence with hers.

Sally did her best to return the kiss with as much passion as she could muster, fumbling her way through what she'd been taught the night before to try and make the kiss as enjoyable for her mistress as it was for her.

When they finally parted, her smile was even brighter and she said with as much determination as she could summon, "I won't fail you, Mistress, you'll see! I *will* do better next time!"

"I know you will, lovely thing." replied Modan, petting what she considered to be the loveliest part of the mage.

Sally squirmed happily over her lap, and then wriggled around so that she could look back at her properly. Now seemed like as good a moment as any to her.

With just a faint hint of trepidation in her voice she said, "Um… I made you something, Mistress."

Swallowing hard, she forced herself to maintain her stare into the naiad's dark eyes.

"I know you can't leave your bog, and I know I can't stay here forever."

At that, she frowned, looking forlorn as if to say that she wished it weren't so.

"But… well… um… since you don't get too many visitors, I thought maybe you might like this to help keep you company…"

Wriggling a little more, she transferred something from her

left hand to her right, and then reached back behind her and opened her palm up to reveal what she'd been clinging to that whole time.

A small pair of crystal figurines, shaped to resemble two women with wide hips and large chests (one taller and more curvaceous than the other, while a red hue suffused the curved bottom of the smaller one) rested on her palm.

"I made them by crystalizing the spring water," she said by way of explanation. "They are in many ways like ice, but the Power of the spring prevents them from melting or being too cold, so they should last for a *very* long time. It took me a while to get the Kura's delights to mix properly with them for the color on my figure, but… well… uh… I um… I hope you like them."

For a very, *very* long moment, Modan was silent.

She just held the crystals in her hand, staring at them with open wonder. It was the first time that Sally had ever seen her honestly at a loss for words.

"You… held on to these. Throughout our whole lesson, and your punishment afterward…"

There was no question there. It was obvious that that was indeed what had happened. Modan blinked, and her liquid eyes seemed suddenly wetter than usual. She continued to hold the figures in her hand, simply staring, and then, almost reluctantly, she raised them up and deposited them into a little spider web supported by two small creepers, which pulled the parcel up into a hollow for safekeeping.

Standing up, Modan pulled Sally up after her to stand on a nearby branch with her, and wrapping her strong arms around the girl's shoulders, she gave her the deepest, most passionate kiss she had ever given in her countless centuries of life.

Sally melted into her arms and returned the kiss as fresh

tears of joy and relief wove hot trails down the sides of her face. She in turn wrapped her arms around her mistress's naked back and clung to her, savoring that moment and etching every single detail of it into her memory as much as she could.

It was one that she knew she would return to many, many times throughout her life.

And it was one that would always make her smile.

Epilogue

– FIVE DAYS LATER –

Modan pulled Sally up from the charax burrow for the last time. She'd been saying her final goodbyes to all of the creatures she'd befriended during her stay in the bog, and the old charax had been the last on her list. She knew that outside of a sacred spring like this one, that animals and plants would be less alive, less personable. But what she'd learned would still help her greatly with them.

Modan hugged and kissed her deeply again, for perhaps the thirtieth time in the still young morning. Her hands cupped the mage's bottom cheeks, which were just as bright red and swollen as they had been pretty much constantly for the past week, and whose most recent beating had happened a mere hour ago. Not for punishment, but simply because Modan had wanted to spank her, and because Sally had wanted to be spanked.

"Your mount is awaiting you at the edge of the path, where you left her. I've ensured her safety, as I promised," said Modan, looking down at Sally, sadly and lovingly, her first true worshipper in the better part of a millennium, and perhaps her most devout of all time.

One of them definitely, at the very least.

"Thank you for everything, Mistress Modan," replied Sally with a watery smile, rising up onto her tiptoes to give the naiad one last quick kiss and doing her best to imprint the taste of her lips on her memory for forever.

Settling back onto her heels with tears in her eyes, she

beamed warmly up at her and added, "I'll *never* forget you!"

She couldn't bring herself to say the actual word "good-bye". Deep down she hoped to one day visit here again when she'd advanced a little farther in her journey to master the Power. So instead she stepped in and hugged her as hard as she could one final time, breathing in deeply the unique, blended scents of mud, blossoms, and now marsh marigolds starting to bloom in Modan's hair that were as much a part of her mistress as her powerful hands, before reluctantly letting her go and turning to leave.

Though it had only been a week, it felt to Sally like she'd been with Modan for a lifetime.

But even then, their time together had been far, far too short.

THE END

More Books by Clarine Klein
(Available on Amazon)

Back to Her Teens
Clarine Klein

Back to Her Teens

Petite and oh so sassy college sophomore Rhen Mathews is being kicked out of her dorms to make room for new students, and is in desperate need of a place to live. And so, when Dana Johnson, her former boss from her brief stint as an assistant at a local daycare, offers to let her move in with her for free, she accepts without a second thought.

The only condition?

She has to do so as her thirteen-year-old niece from out of town.

What follows is a forced regression/ageplay novel filled to the brim with super embarrassing moments for Rhen and lots of much-needed spanking and discipline from her loving, but very strict, Auntie Dana.

Cat and Mouse
ATTITUDE ADJUSTER
Clarine Klein

Cat and Mouse

Cassidy Coleman is a sassy but introverted college sophomore out on her own for the first time in her young adult life. At the start of fall semester, she moves into an apartment with a randomly assigned roommate, Lauren Delaney. Lauren is a an outgoing and athletic economics major one year ahead of Cassidy in school, and is just looking for a place to live that doesn't also double up as a party house on the weekends.

Unfortunately, things start off more than a little awkward between the two of them at first, with Cassidy too tongue-tied by the captivating older girl to carry on more than a two sentence conversation before needing to flee to her bedroom. Eventually though, the two manage to bond over a mutual love of video games from their childhood, and overnight an instant and lifelong friendship is forged. From there friendship then blossoms into love when after pushing her roommate into a freezing pool on a chilly winter night, Cassidy suddenly finds herself being hauled across Lauren's ample lap for a bare bottom blistering they've both been dreaming of for weeks.

And it's only the beginning!

The SPANKING of Sally Marie

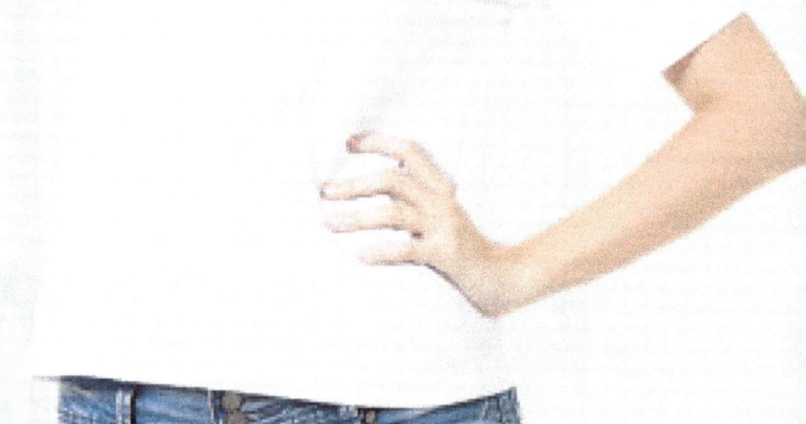

CLARINE KLEIN

The Spanking of Sally Marie

Sally finds herself in trouble once too often, and as grounding and other forms of punishment have had little effect on Sally's bratty behavior, her parents decide to spank their teenage daughter instead. It all begins when Sally stays up half the night playing around on her computer. Her dad is not pleased, and upends her for a bare bottom spanking. It is the first of many such spankings delivered by either Mom or Dad, and things get mega embarrassing for Sally when she's spanked in the Ladies Room in the mall, and in a side room at the local church during the Sunday service. Sally soon finds out the difference between 'attitude adjuster' spankings and the real thing, and her humiliation increases when her girlfriends find out she's still getting spanked - they even seize an opportunity to spank her themselves!

Thank you for reading!